D1039509

MAD WOMAN 2

A Novel By: Lady Lissa

Copyright © 2017 Lady Lissa

Published by Tiece Mickens Presents, LLC

All rights reserved. No part of this book may be reproduced in any form without written consent of the publisher, except brief quotes used in reviews.

This is a work of fiction. Any references or similarities to actual events, real people, living or dead, or to real locals are intended to give the novel a sense of reality. Any similarity in other names, characters, places, and incidents are entirely coincidental.

It's easy to join our mailing list!

Just send your email address by text message:

Text

TMPBOOKS

to 22828 to get started.

Final scene from book one...

Maddie

How the hell could our running into those two be a coincidence? I loved Nova to death, but if I found out that she set me up, I would never forgive her. This was supposed to be a good day for us to get pampered and shit. But instead of getting pampered, I had to run into Lincoln's sister and his wife. I thought she was a bit frumpy and needed a lot more than a massage to make him want her again. Call me naïve or gullible, but that was how I felt. Lincoln told me that he no longer wanted her and I believed him. The two of us were going to be together, no matter what tricks she had up her sleeve.

He didn't want her anymore and the sooner she realized that, the better off they both would be. Once we were placed on the massage tables, it was a little hard for me to relax, but I found a way. I mean, that lady was rolling and tugging and the shit felt good, so relaxing wasn't a problem at all.

"Are you sure you're okay?" Nova asked.

"I'm good. If you thought that was going to keep me away from him, you were wrong, BFF!" I said through clenched teeth.

I didn't want to believe she had set me up, but it did seem like something she might have done. "Wait a minute! Do you think I did this on purpose?" she asked.

"Are you saying that the four of us ending up here was sheer coincidence?" I countered.

"That's exactly what it was. C'mon Maddie, you know me and you know that I've always had your back, no matter what the situation. This shit here is messy and not my style. I resent you thinking that I would even put you in such a position!" she said with a hurtful expression on her face.

Maybe she didn't set me up. Maybe I was overreacting. Maybe I owed my best friend an apology.

"I'm sorry, Nova. You're absolutely right and I'm trippin'."

"Yea, you really are!" she said.

"I said I was sorry."

"We're good. I think that you should have a conversation with him just to make sure the two of you are on the same page," Nova suggested.

"We speak every single day, so you don't have to worry. A conversation will definitely be had as soon as I get back home," I said.

"I just don't want you to get hurt."

"I won't and besides, I'm a big girl. Whatever happens, happens," I said.

We continued our pampering session and three hours later, we walked out the door. I slid in the front seat of Nova's Lincoln MKZ. My phone began to ring, so I pulled it from my bag and answered as soon as I saw Lincoln's name and handsome face pop up.

"Hey you," I answered.

"Hey baby, what you up to? I called you earlier…"

"Yea, me and Nova had come to the spa to get pampered a little," I said.

"Oh yea! What kind of pampering did you do?"

"I got a manicure, pedicure, a relaxing massage and I waxed my kitty," I said as I smile shyly into the phone receiver.

"Damn baby, you just made my dick hard," he said as he laughed.

"I bet I did."

"You have no idea how much I miss you."

"I miss you too," I confessed.

"I can't wait to see you next week."

"I can't wait to see you," I said.

"I wanna make love to you all night and all day for the first three days," he said in a seductive voice.

"That sounds fine with me. How's it going out there?"

"It's going. Working hard and thinking about coming home to you," he said.

"I can't wait until I see you next week."

"I can't wait either. Well, lemme get back to work. I'll call you tonight before I go to bed," Lincoln said.

"Okay, talk to you soon," I said.

"You betcha!" he said and ended the call.

"I guess that was Smoke, huh?" Nova asked.

"Sure was. He said he can't wait to see me next week. To be honest, I'm definitely anxious to see him."

"You didn't mention seeing his wife," she said.

"That's because she ain't nobody. His wife is the furthest person from my mind right now. All I'm worried about is when Lincoln will be making his way back to me. Everything else is irrelevant," I stated. I needed her to know that whatever was going on between Lincoln and his wife did not concern me.

"Okay. I just hope you know what you're doing," Nova stated.

"Does it seem as though I'm confused about what's going on?" I asked.

"No, not at all. You seem quite the opposite."

A few minutes later, we pulled into the parking lot of my apartment complex. I looked over at Nova and said, "Thanks for taking me to the spa today. I'm sorry if I accused you of setting me up, but that's how it seemed. Just know that I appreciate you for being my friend, even when I do some shit that you don't agree with."

"Well, good friends will be honest and keep it real with you. That's all I'm trying to do. I love you, Maddie."

"I love you too. I'll call you later," I said.

****

The following week, I was a nervous wreck waiting for Lincoln to come home. I had missed him so much and I couldn't wait to see him. When I heard my doorbell ringing around five that evening, I rushed to answer it. I pulled the door back and there he stood, looking all cute in his scraggly beard. I didn't care though. Shit, my man had been on an oil rig for 28 damn days. I didn't care if his beard was hung down to his chest and birds were nesting in it.

I jumped up and wrapped my legs and arms around him as we kissed and held each other. He carried me straight to the bedroom, just like I knew he would. We wasted no time getting naked as we began to satisfy each other's hunger. He immediately placed his mouth on my kitty and started sucking and licking. "Mmmmm!" he murmured.

He dipped his fingers in my snatch and my ocean opened up on him. I was so embarrassed, but he didn't seem to care. He continued to lick and feast on my goodies as I watched him. I grinded my pussy into his face as he picked up the pace. He finally made his way to my lips and drove his meaty pole inside me. "Aaaarrrggh sssshhiiitt!" I moaned as he slipped in and out of me slowly.

"I missed you so much," he said.

"I missed you too," I said to him and I really had missed him.

He leaned into me and kissed me hard on the mouth. That kiss was so hot and steamy that my windows fogged up. I wrapped my legs around his waist as he drove into me like a jack hammer. I howled in pleasure, sounding like a wolf in heat. A few minutes later, his body shuddered and he released his orgasm. We lay beside each other and tried to steady our breathing.

"Whew!" I said as I released an exasperated sigh.

"I had been waiting on that pussy for so long I could feel my dick inside you before I even put it in. You got some real good shit, babe," he said as he marveled in the aftermath of our session.

"Well, that's good to know."

He smacked my butt and bit down on my shoulder softly. "You better watch yourself before you start something you can't finish right now," I smiled.

"Bullshit! I promise you if I start it, I'ma finish it," he smiled back. As a matter of fact, don't move!"

"Where are you going?" I asked as he sat up in bed.

He didn't go anywhere. Instead he rubbed his semi hard dick on my ass until I felt him slapping me with it. I knew it had come to life then. I just lay on my stomach the way he told me to. A few seconds later, he parted my butt cheeks and slid his big dick inside me. "Aww damn!" I murmured as he went to work making me feel great again.

That man had my eyes rolling to the back of my damn head. I was making all kinds of noises in that damn apartment. I tried to bury my face in the pillow, but he wanted to hear my moans of pleasure. As he continued to bang my pussy out, I continued to squeal like the little piggy that went to market. I was truly happy that my baby was home.

DING DONG! DING DONG! DING DONG! DING DONG!

Who the fuck was beating on my damn doorbell like they stupid?

Lincoln asked, "You expecting someone?"

"Uh, no! The only person I was expecting is here already," I said.

"I'ma go check. Stay yo fine ass right here."

He smacked my ass as he threw on his boxers and pants. He ran out the room to see what fool was beating on my doorbell. The person was still ringing my bell as he went to answer it. That shit was aggravating as hell. I climbed out of the bed and put my robe on, tying it around my waist. I wanted to know who was at the door also. I prayed it wasn't Nova because if it was, we were going to have a real problem.

When I heard screaming and shouting coming from the front room, I tried to make out the voice. It was a woman and she was yelling at Lincoln.

"What the hell are you doing here, Lincoln?"

"What are you doing here? Did you fuckin' follow me yo?" he asked.

"Why the hell are you here and where are your damn clothes? Are you fuckin' some bitch that lives here?" she asked. "Never mind! I already know the answer to that question! WHERE THE FUCK SHE AT?!"

Then it dawned on me. That person that was beating on my doorbell was his wife. Oh shit! I looked up at the ceiling and said a prayer because I knew shit was about to go down. Ain't no way I was going to allow that woman to walk up in my house and stay in hiding. Hell no! This was my shit and she was about to find out who the fuck I was. I threw on a pair of jogging pants, a t-shirt, and some tennis shoes. I also threw my braids together in a scrunchie and made my way out of my bedroom.

"WHERE YO BITCH AT, LINCOLN?! DAT BITCH KNOW YOU GOT A WIFE?!" she yelled angrily.

"Go home, Tiff. You shouldn't have followed me here," Lincoln said.

"FUCK DAT! WHERE YO BITCH AT?!"

"I'm right here, but I'm far from a bitch," I said as I revealed myself.

"YOU?! YOU'RE THE BITCH THAT'S FUCKIN' MY HUSBAND?!" she asked as her mouth hit the floor. "OH MY GOD! YOU'RE FUCKIN' THE NURSE FROM THE DAMN HOSPITAL!"

"Look, I'm sorry you had to find out about us this way, but I'm gonna need you to refrain from hollering in my house!"

"BITCH, I'MA NEED YOU TO REFRAIN FROM SPEAKING TO ME BEFORE I PUT MY FOOT ALL IN YO TRIFLIN' ASS!" Tiffani said.

"Lincoln, please get her out of my house. I don't have time for this shit!" I stated as I yawned.

"Tiffani, go home!" Lincoln said as he grabbed her by the arm. She yanked her arm from his grasp and said, "I ain't going nowhere without you!"

"YOU WANNA BET?" I asked as I picked up the phone. "If you don't get the hell up outta my house, I will whoop yo ass then call the police to come arrest you for trespassing."

I had no intentions on calling the police. I just wanted her out of my shit before I got some kind of violation from management. She needed to get the hell out of my place.

"You gon' let that bitch talk to me like that?" she asked as she stared at Lincoln.

"I ain't gonna be too many more bitches," I said as I stared at her.

"WOULD YOU PREFER HOMEWRECKER?! THAT'S WHAT THE FUCK YOU ARE!" she yelled.

"Your marriage was already in trouble before I came along. If anyone is wrecking your home, it's probably you."

She tried to dash over to me with anger in her eyes and fists clenched, but Lincoln grabbed her and moved her towards the door. "I can't believe you're doing this to me, to us!" she began to sob.

"I'm sorry, Tiff. Go home. We'll talk about this shit later," Lincoln said.

"You need to come home with me now, Lincoln. If you don't, I will cut up, bleach, and burn every last piece of clothes you have at home," she said.

"You better not touch my shit!"

"TRY ME!" Tiffani said through clenched teeth. Lincoln went to the room and put his shirt on and grabbed his keys and phone. He looked at me on the way out the door. What the fuck?

His wife stood there with a satisfied smirk on her face. As the two of them left my apartment, I felt like shit. How could this shit have happened? I didn't want to fall for a married man, but I did. I didn't want to be going through this shit, but I was. What had I done to make things so bad for myself?

Little did I know, this was just the beginning…

Chapter one

Lincoln

As soon as I got home, I showered, changed, and headed straight to Maddie's place. I had been waiting to get between her legs for four long ass weeks. I needed to break her off some and get some of that good good for myself as well. When I walked in the house, Tiffani was waiting for me. She was ready to talk about us having another baby. That was the furthest thing from my damn mind. I mean, the last time I checked, the doctor still hadn't cleared her for sex. So, what the hell was she trying to have a baby for right now anyway.

I rushed in and breezed past her, placing my bags in the walk-in closet before going into the bathroom to turn on the water. "Well, hello to you too, Lincoln," she said sarcastically.

"I'm sorry, Tiff. Hey, I just got some place that I need to be so I don't have time to really talk right now. How you doing? You good?" I asked as I looked at her.

"Yea, I'm good. I just wanted to talk to you, that's all. I mean, you've been gone for a month and all we did was text each other. I'd like to have a conversation with my husband, if it's all the same to you," she said as she eyed me.

"Sure, we can have a convo…"

"Good."

"First thing tomorrow," I finished. "I got somewhere I really need to be."

"What could be more important than a conversation with YOUR WIFE?!" she asked, putting extra bass in those last two words. I knew she was my wife, but I wasn't trying to hear that shit right now. All I wanted to do was get between Maddie's legs again, that was it. Was that too much to ask? Just a little pussy in my life after not getting any for four long weeks.

As I grabbed my boxers and undershirt from the dresser drawer, I looked at her. "Look Tiff, I don't want to argue with you, but…"

"But, an argument is exactly what we're going to have if you don't tell me what the hell this is about. Why are you leaving? Where are you going that's so damn urgent?" she asked as she peered at me behind her new glasses. That was the first time I noticed those suckas sitting on her face.

"When did you get glasses?" I asked.

"Last week! I sent you a picture. You didn't get it?"

"Nah, I don't recall getting that pic," I said as I made my way to the bathroom.

She followed me and before I could close the door, she had stepped into my personal fucking space. What was it with her? Was she trying to piss me off? If that was her goal, she was going to be disappointed because nothing could piss me off today. I was finally going to get to see Maddie's sexy ass and right about now, she was all that mattered. I looked at Tiffani, who had taken up space on the counter top, her feet dangling off the side.

"Damn! I guess a nigga can't get no privacy to wash his ass, huh?" I asked in a sarcastic tone similar to the one she had earlier.

"Well, we need to talk. If this is the only way you'll listen to me, so be it."

"Actually, once I step into the shower, I won't be able to hear shit so this is going to have to wait. I mean, what the hell is so damn important that you can't wait until tomorrow?"

"Wait until tomorrow? I've been waiting four weeks to have a conversation with MY HUSBAND! And now, you want me to wait another day? HA! I don't think so!" she said as she craned her neck.

"Suit yourself," I said as I stripped out of my clothes and jumped in the shower.

She was talking, but I wasn't listening or trying to answer her. I had one thing on my mind and it wasn't her. As I lathered myself with soap, I could hear her fussing because I wasn't answering her. She was really about to be pissed when I turned this shower radio on, but I told her I wasn't trying to hear none of that shit she was speaking about. I turned the knob on the radio and Cardi B.'s new hit, *Bodak Yellow* was on. I was jamming that shit as I finished my shower.

Next thing I know, the shower door was being opened and in walked Tiff.

"What the fuck are you doing, yo? I can wash my own ass!" I said.

"I told you that we needed to talk. I'm sick and tired of you ignoring me, Lincoln. I don't deserve this shit! I'm a good woman," she said as tears rained down her cheeks.

"You're right. You are a good woman, but this ain't the time or the place to discuss how good a woman you are. Shit, you don't see me interrupting your bath to tell you what a good man I am," I said as I turned the radio and shower off. I slid the door open and climbed out the stall. I didn't know what the hell was going on with my wife, but she was really pissing me off.

She followed me, still bawling her eyes out like a big baby. I was tempted to call her mom to come see about her because this shit that she was doing wasn't normal. And if she wanted to act like a big ass baby, who better to coddle her ass than her mom. I wasn't for that shit. I had a pussy to pop and she wasn't stopping shit.

"Why don't I call your mom to come spend some time with you?" I suggested. "Maybe y'all can go get pedicures or something... my treat."

"I don't want any damn pedicure! I want some time with my damn husband!" she cried.

"Well, that's not going to happen today, no matter how much you whine like a baby," I said.

I dried myself off and stared at my face in the mirror. I could do a quick shave because Lord knows I needed one, but I would get a haircut tomorrow. I had more pressing matters at hand right now, so that haircut and shave would just have to wait. I lathered myself with lotion before rolling the deodorant stick under my arms. I brushed my teeth and continued to watch Tiffani as she watched me in the mirror.

"You ain't got nothing better to do than monitor me?" I asked.

"We need to talk, Lincoln."

I realized I wasn't going to get anywhere unless I gave her what she wanted. I turned around, leaned against the counter, and said, "So talk."

"This isn't a conversation to have while standing in a bathroom. We need to be sitting down," she protested.

Damn! This woman was going to make me regret coming home first. I made my way to the living room and sat down on the recliner. I didn't want to sit on the sofa because I wanted my own damn space. She sat down on the sofa and looked at me. As I winded my finger in and out of my hair, I waited for her ass to say something. I mean, she was so adamant that we talked now what the hell was she waiting for?

"You not gon' say nothing? Because if you ain't I got shit to do!" I said.

"Lincoln, what has happened to us? Where did things go so wrong that we can't even have a conversation?"

"Things aren't so bad that we can't have a conversation. I'm sitting here waiting for you to have the conversation you feel we so desperately need to have today."

"You haven't been the same person for a while. What's changed you?" she asked.

"That's what you wanna talk about? Is this the conversation that can't wait until tomorrow?"

"I want my husband back!" she cried.

"I'm still your husband, but I can't be that man I used to be. This is who I am. I'm sorry you don't like the way that I am, but there's nothing I can do about that," I said.

"I want us to work on our marriage. Maybe we can get some counseling, I just want us to get back right so we can have a family," she said.

Oh shit! I knew that was coming. There was no way the two of us were having any babies up and through here. She needed to understand that shit and move on.

"We're not going to have a family," I stated.

"What?" she asked, her face reflecting her shock.

"I don't want children right now. I think that's why God saw fit to take the last one from you. We aren't ready," I said.

Tears slid down her cheeks as the reality of what I had just said sunk in. "We aren't ready or you're not ready?"

"I'm not ready. I don't want to start a family with you right now, Tiff. Hell, I might never be ready to start a family with you! I wish you would just get that through your head so we can move past this issue." I stated.

"Is there someone else?" she asked softly.

"What?"

"Are you seeing someone else? I need you to be honest with me, Lincoln."

"I gotta be fuckin' someone else to not want to have a family with you? Is that it?" I asked. "That's not why I don't want us to have kids. I don't want us to have kids because our whole relationship is fucked up. I've told you that so many times before the miscarriage. Bringing a child into the world right now would be selfish on our part because our marriage is already in trouble. Why put an innocent baby through some fucked up shit that we're going through?" I asked as I shook my head.

"Our marriage is in trouble because you've given up on us. I guess your new bitch has your nose wide open somewhere else, so it's fuck me! I love you, Lincoln. What can I do to make this better?" she asked.

I would be an idiot if I said I didn't give a fuck. The truth was, I hated seeing her like that. I never meant to hurt her, but our marriage was over. The only reason I didn't come right out and tell her that was because I knew she was still grieving over the miscarriage she had weeks ago. As soon as enough time passed, I was going to let her know that we needed to get a divorce. I didn't see any reason to stay in a loveless marriage, especially when I wanted another woman.

"I don't know how we can make this better. Look, I gotta go, but we can talk about this tomorrow."

With that being said, I stood up from my seat and walked back into the bedroom to finish getting dressed. She followed me once again, trying to have another conversation. I wasn't having it this time though. I had already wasted almost two hours of my time with her. I finished getting myself together, grabbed my wallet, phone and keys, and said, "Don't wait up."

"So you're sleeping out again?"

"Maybe…"

I walked out the house and jumped in my truck. I was a happy muthafucka to finally be out of the house and on my way to Maddie's. Just thinking about having sex with her had my dick doing flip flops in my damn draws. Shit, I couldn't get over there fast enough. Had I paid attention, I would have known my wife was behind me and I could have derailed that train before it crashed. But, I was so engrossed in my own thoughts, I had completely forgotten about her once I left the house.

Chapter two

Tiffani

I was so excited that my husband was coming home today. I had planned this day for the entire week. I had taken off from work just to stay home and cook his favorite meal and spend time with him. It was almost one thirty in the afternoon when he finally made it home, but that didn't matter. The meatloaf was still juicy and the potatoes were fluffy. I had some dinner rolls in the oven and a salad in the fridge. I had planned for this to a tee.

When he walked in, without so much as a hello, I wondered what was going on. The way he was zipping through the house, you would have sworn there was a fire in the building. I watched him place his bags in the closet and head for the bathroom. I was standing there like, hello! It was as if I wasn't even in the room because he completely ignored me.

I followed him in the bathroom because I wanted to know what was going on. I just couldn't understand what the big rush or emergency was. Then he told me that he wasn't even going to be home tonight. He was getting ready to get out of here and we could talk tomorrow. Why did we have to talk tomorrow? Why couldn't he take the time to talk to me now? After all, I was his wife.

The conversation we had was dry as fuck and we didn't get anywhere. I loved my husband and I really wanted our marriage to work, but he wasn't giving me anything positive. After trying to have a conversation with him for about an hour, it was evident to me that wherever he had to go was more important than me and our marriage.

That was kind of hard for me to accept because I put Lincoln first all the time. I would never put anyone else before him because he was the one I was closest to. I vowed to love, honor and cherish him and I planned to do just that.

I didn't know why he didn't take our vows as seriously as I did. The fact that he couldn't wait to get away from me had my radar all the way up. I knew that my husband was cheating on me. What other reason would he be acting the way that he was? The difference between him and my ex was that I wasn't married to my ex. He cheated on me more than once and I finally dumped his trifling ass. But, I couldn't just dump my husband. We had said vows before our friends and family. We had a commitment to each other and whether he wanted it or not, he was stuck with me.

When I was unable to convince him to stay with me, I just threw up my hands in surrender. Once he left, I was beside myself. How the hell could he just leave me at home alone? He had been gone for almost a month, yet he still couldn't wait to get somewhere else. I knew he had to have another woman. I just knew it. About an hour after he left, I got a phone call that put everything in perspective. Now I knew why he couldn't wait to get out the house. Now I knew why he was in such a rush to leave me by myself. I ended the phone call, grabbed my purse and keys, and headed out the door.

I put the address that I was given into the navigation system and forty minutes later, I pulled into the parking lot to a luxury apartment complex. The complex was beautiful and one of the newer buildings. Whoever lived here definitely had to paying a pretty steep price. The lawns were perfectly manicured, the bushes neatly trimmed and the beautiful fountain at the entrance was truly inviting. I wondered what bitch lived here and prayed that the caller was wrong about my husband.

Of course, in the back of my mind, I already knew she wasn't lying. I knew that whatever bitch lived here was the one that was fucking my husband. I couldn't believe that my husband was cheating on me, even though he swore he wasn't. I parked my car a few spots away from where his truck was parked and took a deep breath. I couldn't believe I was about to confront my husband and come face to face with his bitch.

I slipped out of the car and slowly made my way to the apartment, 36A. I was standing outside of the apartment, ready to ring the bell when I heard loud moans and screams coming from the other side of the door. I put my ear closer to the door and literally got sick to my stomach. The idea of my husband fucking some other bitch had always been a factor in my mind. But, actually hearing it going down was something totally different. I turned around and started puking right there near her doorstep.

"Are you okay?" came a voice behind me.

Hell no, I wasn't okay! My husband was in that apartment fucking some random bitch! That was the response I wanted to give, but of course, I couldn't say that. I just wiped the sides of my mouth and nodded my head. "I'll be fine," I said weakly.

"Are you sure?" the voice asked again.

"Yes, I'm fine," I lied.

I was anything but fine right now. How could this be happening to me again? What had I done that was so bad that men kept cheating on me? I was a good woman; I worked, I cooked, I kept the house clean and I fucked my husband regularly. Well, lately we hadn't been engaging in sex because of the miscarriage and he had left to go to work.

The person finally left me alone and I pressed my ear to the door again. The moans had subsided, but then it started back up again. They must have me fucked all the way up. I started ringing the shit out of that doorbell now. That bitch was getting all the dick that should have been mine. My husband was all up inside her when it should have been me he was giving it to. How could he betray me that way? How could he betray our vows?

I continued to ring the bell until he finally opened the door. The surprised look on his face matched mine as I stared at him in his pants only.

"What are you doing here?" he asked through clenched teeth. I could tell that he was trying to get rid of me without the bitch finding out, but that wasn't going to happen like that.

"WHAT AM I DOING HERE?! YOU'RE FUCKIN' KIDDING ME, RIGHT?!" I yelled angrily.

"Keep your voice down!"

"I WILL NOT KEEP MY VOICE DOWN! WHAT ARE YOU DOING HERE?! IS THIS WHY YOU COULDN'T SPEND THE NIGHT WITH YOUR WIFE? BECAUSE YOU'RE OVER HERE FUCKING SOME TWO BIT WHORE!" I was so hurt and angry. I hoped people in this complex heard me. They deserved to know that they were living next door to a trifling bitch so these wives could watch their husbands.

"Tiffani, how did you find me? What the hell are you doing here?" he asked as he looked back at the bedrooms.

"WHERE'S THAT BITCH?! HUH? WHERE IS SHE?!" I screamed.

"Tiff please, go home! We can talk about this later!"

"WHERE YO BITCH AT THOUGH, LINCOLN?! DAT BITCH KNOW YOU GOT A WIFE?!"

"Go home, Tiff. You shouldn't have followed me here," Lincoln said.

"FUCK DAT! WHERE YO BITCH AT?!"

"I'm right here, but I'm far from a bitch." I heard the words and the voice sounded familiar, but it couldn't be who I thought it was. I turned around and saw the bitch that had taken care of me in the hospital that day I lost my baby. What the hell was really going on here? My husband was fucking the nurse! This had to be a fucking dream, well, a nightmare.

"YOU?! YOU'RE THE BITCH THAT'S FUCKIN' MY HUSBAND?!" I asked as I tried to keep myself from running up on her ass. I had to remember that I was in her house and could go to jail if I kicked her ass in this house. "OH MY GOD! YOU'RE FUCKIN' THE NURSE FROM THE DAMN HOSPITAL!"

I was in total shock and disbelief. This bitch tended to me during one of the hardest times in my life. Yet, here she was now, fucking my husband. It took everything in me not to slap the shit out of her.

"You need to come home with me now, Lincoln. If you don't, I will cut up, bleach, and burn every last piece of clothes you have at home," I said.

"You better not touch my shit!" he said.

"TRY ME!" I said through clenched teeth.

I walked out and he followed behind me a few minutes later. I couldn't believe this shit was happening to me again. As I made my way down the walkway, I noticed people coming out of their apartments trying to see what the commotion was about.

"IF YOU'RE A MARRIED WOMAN LIVING NEXT TO THAT BITCH IN 36A, WATCH OUT FOR YOUR HUSBANDS! SHE WILL FUCK HIM BEHIND YOUR BACK WHILE SMILING IN YO DAMN FACE! HIDE YO HUSBANDS, LADIES! THE BITCH IN 36A IS A HOMEWRECKER!!" I yelled.

As my husband followed behind me angrily, he hissed, "Will you stop? You're making a fool of yourself!"

I turned around, stopping him dead in his tracks with the look on my face. How dare he leave me at home to come over here and fuck that bitch! Then, tell me that I'm making a fool out of myself. The fucking nerve of him! I hauled off and slapped the shit out of him.

WHAP!

I raised my finger in his face and said, "How dare you tell me some shit like that! IF I LOOK LIKE A FOOL, IT'S BECAUSE OF YOU, NOT ME! YOU MADE ME LOOK LIKE A FOOL!" By that time, tears were spilling from my eyes. I had never been so hurt or embarrassed in my entire life. I turned on my heels and headed for my car. I was so angry.

I knew that my husband was in the wrong for sleeping with that THOT nurse, but she was just as much to blame. People always said that the woman shouldn't blame the other bitch because her husband was the one that fucked up. After all, he was the one that owed it to me to remain loyal. But still, that bitch heard me talking about getting ready for my man to come home and she turned around and seduced him. I was so mad that I had to inhale, exhale, and scream before I finally pulled out of the parking lot. I couldn't believe that this shit was happening.

As my husband got in his truck, I could tell that he was upset. Did I give a fuck? Hell no! I didn't give two shits how he felt. I knew damn well he didn't care how I felt otherwise; he wouldn't have disrespected me that way. I burned out of the parking lot and checked the rearview to make sure he was following behind me. I was not looking forward to the argument we were about to have, but it was inevitable.

I parked in the driveway and jumped out of the car. I unlocked the front door and he followed me inside.

"What the hell were you thinking following me?" he fumed.

I wondered if he was serious because I had just caught him in the act of fucking another bitch and he was mad at me for following him. He had to be kidding me.

"You have some nerve. You're upset with me for following you, but you disrespected our vows! How could you do that?" I cried. "I mean, I had a feeling you weren't happy, but to do this. Obviously, the vows we took on our wedding day meant nothing to you."

"I'm sorry that you had to find out this way. I didn't mean for you to find out like this," he said.

"YOU DIDN'T MEAN FOR ME TO FIND OUT LIKE THAT?! IS THAT ALL YOU HAVE TO SAY?!" I asked.

"What else can I say? I told you I was sorry," he repeated.

"Why are you sorry, though? Are you sorry because you hurt me, or because I found out? What exactly are you sorry about, Lincoln?"

"I'm just sorry about everything."

"You should be!"

"I don't know what else you want me to say."

"There's nothing else you can say. I just don't understand how you could do this to me… to us and our marriage. I told you on more than one occasion how much I love you and want to work this out. You said you wanted our marriage to work, but obviously, you lied. I just don't understand what I did wrong," I cried.

I didn't want to cry. I didn't want to feel this way and be all broken up inside, but how could I not? I didn't want him to see that I was vulnerable and I definitely didn't want him to feed me a bunch of bullshit. I loved my husband, but I didn't want to hear anymore lies.

He walked over to me and took me in his arms. At first, I tried to push him away. I didn't want him touching me after he was just touching that bitch. But, I knew if I did that he would go right back to her and that was something I didn't want. I wanted my husband and the life we once had. We were once happy and I knew we could be that way again. We had to make this work. I had plans for us to have a family together. How could we do that if we weren't together?

"I love you, Lincoln. I want us to have a happy marriage, even if it means we have to go to counseling. I'm willing to do that. Are you?" I asked him as I looked up at him.

He hesitated a little, but then he said, "I suppose we could work on our marriage."

"No, you have to be all in. Saying shit like 'I suppose' means you might stray again. I won't be with you if you're going to continue cheating with that bitch!" I said.

"Fine, we'll go to counseling and try to make our marriage work," he relented.

"Thank you."

His phone started to ring and I looked at him. "Aren't you gonna answer it?"

"Nah."

"I think you should change your number."

"I'm not doing that. I use my phone for business reasons so…"

"Well, you need to tell her not to call you anymore," I said.

"You wanna make this marriage work or not? Because if you do, you can't keep bringing up what happened tonight. You have to be able to forgive me and move past it," he said.

How the hell was I supposed to do that when it just happened? I just caught them having sex so how did he expect me to move on from that just like that. But, if it would help me get my marriage back on track, I was going to try.

Little did I know that what happened tonight was going to be like déjà vu…

Chapter three

Maddie

How did that bitch find out that Lincoln was here? I couldn't believe that he just left with her. He said he was going to leave her. Yet, when she showed up here, he tucked his tail between his legs and left with her. We were supposed to be together. That was what he promised me. How could that shit have happened?

The nerve of her to even show up at my house in the first place. I mean, I didn't owe her shit and if she thought her man was cheating on her ass, she should have addressed it when he went back home. To show up here and make a scene in front of my neighbors was ridiculous. Now she had these women looking at me crazy, as if I wanted their husbands. I didn't want their men. I wanted Lincoln.

After him and his wife left, I picked up the phone and called the only person I could talk to about this.

"Hey BFF, what's up?"

"You will never guess what happened here tonight," I said.

"What girl?"

"Well, Lincoln came by here when he got back from the rig."

"I did not need to hear that. I mean, you heard his wife making plans for them when he got back. Why would you stick yourself in such a messy situation?"

"I didn't call for any advice, Nova. I just need you to listen," I said.

"Fine, I'll listen. But can I say something first?"

"What?" I asked as I rolled my eyes.

"He's married and I just want you to remember that so you don't get hurt," she said.

"Thanks, Nova but I'm a big girl. I know how to take care of myself."

"Fine. Do you then, big girl," Nova said. I could tell she was upset, but I didn't care because I didn't need her telling me how to run my relationship. She had the perfect relationship with Josiah so she would never understand what I was going through.

"I wanted to tell you what happened earlier, but now I'm not so sure I should. You seem to have it in your mind that everything I do is wrong. I'll just talk to you later," I said.

"Wait! I'm sorry if it seems as if I was passing judgment on you. You're right. I'm your best friend and you're mine. If there's something you want to talk about, I'm here to listen," Nova said.

It was too late though. I didn't have shit to say anymore because I was already upset. "That's okay. We'll talk some other time." I said.

I ended the call after that. I dialed Lincoln's number, but he didn't answer. I called again, but still no answer. I decided to go take a shower. When I was done, I dried myself off and climbed in the bed. The cool, satin sheets felt good against my bare skin. I decided that after what happened tonight and the fact that Lincoln was ignoring me, I would move on. I wasn't going to deal with him anymore. He could keep his wife, if that was who he wanted.

****

Three months later...

For the past three months, all I did was work hard and spend time with my mom. I did my best to do everything possible to avoid Lincoln and anything to do with him. The last thing I needed was the drama that had transpired that night his wife showed up at my place. I hadn't seen or spoken to him since that night and I was fine with that. Nova and I still spent time together, but I tried my best to avoid gatherings where I knew Lincoln would be present. I missed him so much, but what could I do about it?

Unless he came to me and said they were separated or they had filed for divorce, it just didn't make sense to continue what we started. He had obviously made the decision to stay with her so I was going to step aside and let them handle their business.

But why oh why, did I have to run into them at the grocery store. If I could have turned and run out the store, I would have, but I was here because I needed groceries. I had a basket that was halfway filled and I wasn't going to leave it because of the two of them. Tiffani rolled her eyes at me and grabbed Lincoln's arm. Like, I realized he was her husband and I didn't want to mess with him anymore. She could have her cheating ass husband.

As I continued to walk towards them, my eyes locked with his. I tried to look away, but I couldn't tear my gaze from his. Tiffani looked from him to me before saying, "Take a picture, it'll last longer."

"I don't need a picture," I responded with an attitude.

"Well, the way you're looking at my husband…"

"What about the way your husband is looking at me? You should check your man!" I said as I brushed past them.

As I continued to do my shopping, I could hear the two of them arguing on the next aisle. I smiled in satisfaction at the fact that they were arguing. That's what the fuck she gets for trying to call me out. I made my way to the checkout register and paid for my groceries. By the time I had made it outside, the two of them were headed out, no groceries in hand and involved in a full-blown argument. That was the icing on the cake. As long as Lincoln was married to her, he would never get any peace.

His wife was so insecure, but she had a reason to be the way that she was though. Her husband was a liar and a cheater. She obviously didn't mind that he cheated on her. When I decided I was ready for another relationship, I was going to make sure that man was all mine.

I got all my groceries put away then went to take a quick shower. I had just stepped out the shower when I heard my doorbell ringing. I wrapped the towel around me and went to answer it. I pulled the door open and there stood Lincoln, looking as good as ever. I tried to act like I didn't care why he was here, but my heart was beating so fast and furious, I just knew he could see it thumping through my towel. That was when I realized how underdressed I was.

"Why are…"

Before I could get the words out, he pushed me inside the apartment, closed the door, and pinned me against the wall. His lips covered mine in an instant as my blood rushed to my head, leaving me lightheaded. I wrapped my arms around him and welcomed the love he was about to give me. My towel dropped to the floor as did his pants and boxers. He wasted no time penetrating me with his meaty stick.

I sucked in a deep breath as he wrapped my legs around his waist and pummeled inside me. I felt an orgasm reaching the surface as my body shuddered. I held onto him as he continued to show me how much he missed me. He held my butt cheeks in his hand as he pumped in and out of me. "I love you, Maddie. I never stopped loving you," Lincoln muttered in my ear as he kissed my earlobe.

It felt so good to hear him tell me that he loved me and never stopped. I grabbed him by both sides of his face and looked at him in the eyes. "Are you sure?"

He gave it to me again, deep and steady strokes. "Yea. I'll always love you," he said.

"I love you too," I said, realizing I meant every word.

His strokes got deeper and hit my G-spot with such force, I thought my back would split. He continued to pump inside me, over and over again. It was like we were making up for lost time in years instead of months. We hadn't been together for three months, but the love he was giving me was at least a year's worth. I cringed and shivered as my body succumbed to another orgasm. Finally, after about two hours, Lincoln came. The moan he made came from deep within. I could tell that he was satisfied.

He slowly let me down on my feet, but my knees were wobbly and shaky. I leaned against him as we walked to my bedroom. I sat down on the bed and he sat next to me. "What happens now?" I asked as I tried to steady my breathing.

"What do you mean?" he asked.

"I mean, where do we go from here? I don't want to be the side chick again. If you aren't going to leave your wife…"

"I have no problem leaving my wife. Frankly, I'm tired of this shit we call a marriage. That woman has been putting me through hell since she found out about us and I think it might be best if I file for a divorce. I tried to make things work with her, but it's too damn hard. Marriage shouldn't be that hard."

"Oh my God! Are you serious? I mean, are you sure?" I asked.

"Hell yea, I'm sure! You have no idea what I've been going through. I love you, Maddie. Are you sure that I'm what you want? I mean, if I file for divorce, are you sure you'll want to be with me? I'm just trying to make sure that it's not the excitement of fucking a married man is what's got you."

"Fucking a married man isn't exciting for me. It's degrading, if you want to know the truth. I don't want to be your side chick. I can't do that again, Lincoln. I won't do that again. I deserve more and so do you. If you don't love your wife, maybe you should file for divorce. I love you and I want to be with you," I said.

"You make it sound so simple, baby."

"Why can't it be that simple? Y'all don't have any kids together, so what makes it so hard?" I asked.

"I don't think it's hard. I worry about my wife sometimes, ya know? She used to be so confident, but lately she's been so weak. I just don't want her doing nothing stupid," he said.

"Stupid like what, Lincoln?"

He grabbed me and pulled me on top of him. I could feel his hardness beneath me, which meant he was ready to end our conversation. I didn't want to end it like that, but I had no choice. I slid on his pole and felt it all the way to my stomach. As I bounced on it while kissing him, I realized just how much I had missed him. Sure, I was wrong for sleeping with him again while he was married, but that wasn't my fault. He showed up at my place. I didn't call him or text him or anything.

As we continued to satisfy each other, his phone began to ring. I already knew who it was and prayed she didn't show up at my damn door again. If she did that, I had no problem fighting her ass for disrespecting my place. I lived here and had to deal with the looks my neighbors gave me, not her. If she ever showed up at my place again, it was on and poppin'. Whatever issues she and her husband had should be handled between them.

"Aaarrgghhh! That feels so good!" I cried as he pummeled his big dick inside my warm opening. My pussy hadn't been penetrated in so long that it clung to his dick for dear life. As we continued to ravish each other, his phone continued to ring. After a while, I just blocked it out.

Even though the ringing persisted, I was lost in my own little dream world. Lincoln flipped me onto my back and lifted my leg on his shoulder, plowing deeper inside me. I didn't know how I managed without him these past three months, but I wouldn't go without him any longer. If he wasn't worried about his wife, why should I? Divorce or no divorce, Lincoln loved me and I loved him. We belonged together. He should have never married that woman in the first place.

He began to slow grind inside me, which made my toes curl and my insides shiver. It almost felt as if my insides were frozen. "Oooouuuu! Oh my God!" I cried out. "Ssssss!"

A few minutes later, my doorbell was ringing. "Oh no!" I uttered.

"Sssshhhh!" Lincoln said as he kissed me.

BANG! BANG! BANG! DING DONG! DING DONG!

There was no escaping this. We already knew who it was at the door, but Lincoln continued to get it in. It was like he wasn't even worried about the fact that his crazy wife was at my door again. He just continued to ignore the door and pummeled into me some more. At long last, he finally came. I was so exhausted from the workout we just had, but the ringing and banging on my door continued. "Are you gonna handle that?" I asked him.

"Hell naw! Eventually, she gon' get tired and take her ass home."

Tiffani was now screaming for us to open the door. "She's bringing attention that I don't need at my residence. If I get put out, I will kick her ass!" I said through clenched teeth.

"She'll go away in a little while. Just watch," he said.

"I hope you're right because the last thing I want is to move from here. I'm very happy in my apartment," I said.

"I know and don't worry, she'll be gone soon."

"Lincoln, we gotta talk though. I can't have your wife coming over here every time you decide to leave your house," I said. "I have neighbors and they're nosy as fuck. I don't need these people thinking that I'm just trying to break up your happy home. If that was the case, you wouldn't be here."

"I know and I'm sorry about that. I'll talk to her about that shit. In the meantime, I better get dressed and go deal with her." He slid out the bed and began putting his clothes on. When he was done, he bent down to kiss me. He slid his tongue into my mouth as the kiss grew deeper. He finally pulled back and said, "I love you, Maddie."

"I love you too," I said.

He grabbed his phone and walked out the bedroom. I heard the front door close a few seconds later as I lay back on my pillow. I couldn't believe that I was back in this situation again. My kitty throbbed at the thought of Lincoln putting it down on me. I touched it to try and calm her down. I snuggled next to the pillow that Lincoln had laid his head on for the rest of the night.

Chapter four

Nova

I had a feeling that Maddie and Smoke had hooked back up together. I was hoping that after Tiffani had showed up at her place that first night, she would let him go. I knew that Maddie was my best friend and that my loyalty should have lied with her, but I couldn't help it. I hated when women messed with married men and vice versa. If people are married, others should respect those boundaries and not cross those lines. Maddie was too smart and beautiful to be creeping around with Smoke.

Thinking back to that night, I remembered it as clear as if it had happened last night.

I had called Maddie and she answered the phone all out of breath and shit. I heard Smoke in the background telling her to hang up the phone, which she did. I couldn't believe that he was over there when he had just got home. He should have been with his wife. I excused myself from my comfortable spot in Josiah's arms to make the phone call I knew would end my friendship with Maddie if she ever found out.

"Hello," Tiffani answered.

"Tiff, it's Nova. Is Smoke there?"

"No, he isn't."

"Do you know where he is?" I asked.

"No, I don't. I can tell him that you called when he comes back," she said.

I decided right then that I was going to help her save her marriage. She was obviously clueless when it came to her man. I thought about the fact that I would be betraying my best friend, but she deserved better than Smoke's cheating ass. She deserved a man who would love her and be there for her when she needed him. Not a half of a man who had to split his time between her and his wife. Tiffani would always have the upper hand since she was his wife.

"I think I know where he is," I insinuated.

"What? You know where my husband is?"

"I think so."

"How would you know where MY husband is?"

I just have a feeling. Take this address down," I said as I rattled off Maddie's address. "Apartment 36A."

"Is he with another woman?" she asked.

"Just go there and please, keep this between us," I said as I ended the call. I went back to join Josiah and he was waiting for me. We spent the entire night making up for lost time, all thoughts of Maddie and Smoke gone from my mind.

The next day, Maddie called and asked if we could meet up at the spa again. I agreed because I was anxious to find out if Tiffani had gone there the night before. As we greeted each other, we were led to the massage room. The tranquil atmosphere immediately took away any stress I was feeling. As we were laid face down on the comfortable tables, she began to tell me about her nightmarish night.

"You will never guess what happened last night," she said.

"You're right. I'll probably never guess so why don't you tell me," I said.

"Girl, Lincoln's wife showed up at my apartment!"

"What?!" I asked, pretending to be shocked. "You have got to be kidding me."

"I wish I was kidding! She showed up at my place banging on the door like she was the got damn police! I didn't know who was at my damn door."

"Oh my God! What happened?"

"Well, she was arguing with Lincoln, since he went to get the door, and kept referring to me as a bitch. So, I made my presence known. Then she turned her anger on me!"

"Oh my! Please don't tell me y'all fought," I said.

I wanted Tiffani to find out about her and Smoke, but I would have never forgiven myself if Tiffani had attacked her.

"No, nothing like that, but we did argue."

"How did she know where you lived?" I asked.

"I think she followed him there," she said.

"So, what happened?"

"Well, she threatened to bleach and burn all his clothes if he didn't leave with her, so they left together."

"Wow! Sounds like you had the night from hell."

"I really did."

"So, are you going to keep seeing Smoke?"

"Hell no! That bitch was yelling outside my apartment that the women needed to watch their husbands because I was a homewrecker and shit! You don't know how bad I wanted to punch her in the face!"

"Well, you can't really blame her, Maddie. I mean, you were sleeping with her husband," I stated.

"So what! Her beef shouldn't be with me, but with her man. He's the one married to her, not me. I don't owe her shit!" she said, surprising me that she would feel that way.

I thought I knew my best friend, but apparently, I missed something. I thought I knew her so well.

"Right, you don't owe her anything, but I just never thought you would want to be someone's side chick. I mean, you had the opportunity to date Smoke long time ago, before he was married. Why wait until he's married to start sleeping with him?" I asked.

"You know, if I didn't know any better, I would think that you had sent his wife to my apartment," she said as she eyed me suspiciously.

"What?!" I shrieked and let out a nervous laugh. I didn't want Maddie to ever find out that I was the one who called Tiffani and told her where she could find Smoke. I mean, that would destroy our friendship.

"Well, the way that you're acting."

"Girl, don't be silly. I just feel that you shouldn't be messing with Smoke because he's married. You deserve to have your own man, not one that you will have to share," I said.

"I suppose you're right."

We made small talk about other stuff for the remainder of our visit at the salon. When we were done, we gave each other goodbye hugs and went our separate ways. I kind of felt bad about the part I played in what happened last night, but Maddie would thank me later. She really deserved better.

Present day…

So, here we were, after getting another round of lovemaking in. I was totally exhausted because Josiah was like a machine when it came to giving me the dick. I never had a man that could put it down the way that he did. He was insatiable when it came to pleasing and satisfying me. As I laid beside him and rubbed my butt against his dick, it slowly came alive. Next thing I knew, we were humping like rabbits. He was slamming into me from behind. He had me screaming like a banshee in my house. That boy had some good dick and he definitely knew how to keep me satisfied.

I wondered if Josiah would ever propose to me. I wanted to get married to him, but after seeing the shit that Smoke and Tiffani were going through, I wondered if I should even bring up the subject. He and Smoke were best friends, so if Smoke had regrets about marrying Tiffani, I didn't want that to rub off on my man if we ever tied the knot. When and if Josiah ever proposed to me, I wanted it to be a forever thing. I didn't want him to ever have a reason to cheat on me. I loved that boy with everything in me…

"Oooouuu! Yea, right there," I moaned as he grinded into me from behind. He bit softly on my neck, causing my clit to throb and my insides to quiver. That was one of my weak spots.

He continued to plow into me as I continued to scream in pleasure. "Oh God! That feels sooooooo good!" I yelled.

"Turn over!" he said as he pulled out.

I knew exactly how he wanted it. I got on my hands and knees, arched my back, and tooted my butt in the air. He got behind me and slid his hot tongue down the slit of my ass cheeks, invading my booty hole. I cringed and shuddered as I gripped the sheets with both hands. "Mmmmmm!" he mumbled from behind as he licked between the hot, wet creases of my purring kitty cat.

My knees were wobbling as he licked up and down and all around. His tongue slid in and out of my wet folds as he sopped up all my juices. "Ssshhhhiittt!" I cried out.

He smacked my ass and tapped it with his hard shaft. I made my ass cheeks jiggle as I waited for him to put his dick inside me. The wait was killing me because I wanted him so badly. "Put it in me, baby… pleeeeeeaaasssseeee!" I begged.

"You want me to put it in?" he asked as he smacked my ass again.

"Yaaaasssss! Pleeeeaaasssseee!" I cried out again.

He rubbed his big mushroom head against the opening of my love well and I tried to back my pussy against it. I wanted him so bad. He finally put me out of my misery and thrusted inside me really hard. His dick slammed against my G-spot, immediately causing my orgasm to burst all over him. He squeezed my fat ass cheeks in each hand as he pummeled my insides. I was delirious with happiness and good feelings. I felt like that fat kid who loved cake in that 50 Cent song.

My man plowed into me, over and over again. I was dizzy with the various feelings I had inside me. Oh God. I didn't know sex could be this good, especially when you've been with someone for longer than four years. I never thought our relationship would last this long. I thought he was a playa, but as it turned out, Smoke was the playa. I thank God every day that he showed interest in Maddie that day and not me.

"Fuck me! FUCK ME!" I screamed as he picked up the pace and really started banging me out. My kitty was gonna be so sore when we were done, but I didn't care.

"Oh shit! I'm about to cum!" he said.

"Cum for me, baby! Cum for me, zaddy!" I cried as he plowed deeper and harder. A few minutes later, he let out a guttural howl and slammed once more in my backside.

"Ooooouuuuu!" I cried as we collapsed beside each other in the bed.

"Damn! You got some good pussy, bae!" he said as he kissed me.

"Mmmmm!" I moaned as I returned his tongue kiss. We finally broke apart and lay stiff and still next to each other. I was breathing so hard and fast, you could have sworn I was running the 400 yard dash.

"Have I told you how much I loved you?" I asked as I laid my head on his chest.

He stroked my hair and said, "Yea, but you can tell me again."

"I love you soooooo much!"

"I love you too, babe."

"Have you heard from Smoke?" I asked him.

"Nah, we supposed to hook up tomorrow though. That gives us just enough time to give our women what they been missing while we been gone," he said.

"Well, on behalf of all the women y'all left behind, thank y'all for that," I said with a laugh.

"You ain't gotta thank me. All you gotta do is open up whenever I'm ready."

He laughed at that and so did I. I had been missing my man this past month. I hated when he left, but he made good money at his job so I sure didn't want him to quit. I worked also as a paralegal for a prominent attorney in the area. I loved my job and was learning so much. My boss was pretty cool too. She usually gave me the first day that Josiah returned off so we could spend some time together.

"I have no problem with that," I said as I kissed him. "Babe, do you know if Smoke and Maddie are still seeing each other?"

"Nah, last I spoke to him, they hadn't been seeing each other. They hadn't seen one another since Tiff had shown up at Maddie's place that night. Smoke is still trying to figure out how she found out where he was."

"I thought you said she followed him there," I said.

"That's what he thought, at first. He said there was no way she could have followed him because she would have followed him inside. He said that Tiff's temper wouldn't have let her stay outside that long," Josiah said.

"Hmmm! Maybe she was just waiting to catch them actually doing something."

There was no way I wanted them to find out that I had sent Tiffani knocking on Maddie's door. I had a lot of time to think about that night and the more I thought about it, the more I realized that I should have kept my big mouth closed. If Maddie ever found out, she would kill me and I couldn't blame her.

"Maybe. Smoke knew better than that. If he wanted to fuck with Maddie that way, he should have done it long time ago. Why wait until he's married to do some shit like that? He should've known that shit would catch up to him."

"If you ever decide to cheat on me, please just break up with me. I don't think I could handle it if you cheated on me like I didn't matter."

"You'll always matter to me, baby. I wouldn't cheat on you because you handle yo shit! I mean, we communicate with one another and that's huge for me. I don't usually like discussing my feelings and shit. But, you make me wanna be a better person for you. You make me wanna do all the right things and shit," he said. I couldn't believe how open he was about his feelings. I lifted my head off his chest and kissed him.

"I'm glad you feel that way, babe. You also make me a better person. I just love you so much," I said.

"I love you too."

He squeezed me tight as he kissed my forehead. We fell into a comfortable silence and a few minutes later, I heard him snoring. I smiled and closed my eyes too. I knew when he would wake up, it would be on and poppin' again so I needed my rest. I fell asleep thinking how lucky I was to have such a wonderful man in my life. I hoped that Maddie would find her Prince Charming one day so she could get her happily ever after. She needed to leave Smoke's ass alone because he definitely was not her prince. Not by a long shot…

Chapter five

Lincoln

I had no plans to see Maddie again because I had promised my wife that I would stay away from her and concentrate on our marriage. The past three months, I had kept that promise and hadn't seen Maddie. My wife and I went to counseling twice a week while I was home and she assumed things were getting better between us. However, I knew they weren't getting better. I tried really hard to love her the way she needed me to, but I couldn't get my mind off Maddie.

You would think, out of sight, out of mind. That wasn't the case. Even though I hadn't been seeing her that didn't take the longing I felt for her away. She just got me, ya know? She made me feel so good when we made love, my fucking toes curled. I really felt that she and I belonged together and no amount of time away from each other was going to change that. But, since I hadn't seen her I was doing my best to stay away and try to make my marriage work.

When I saw her at the grocery store, my dick immediately got hard. My insides started jumping and my heart began to beat faster. I couldn't take my eyes off her, even though my wife was standing right beside me. I tried to look away, but I couldn't help myself.

When Tiff caught the two of us looking at each other, of course she jumped on Maddie. Once Maddie left the aisle that we were on, she laid into me. I wasn't for all that shit in public, so rather than argue with her, I left. To me, anything she had to say to me concerning me and

Maddie should have waited until we were in private. But, Tiffani couldn't wait.

"Why the hell were you looking at her?! Do you still want her?!" she fumed.

"Now is not the time to be discussing this. We can finish this discussion at home," I said.

I continued to push the cart, but she kept fussing with me. I just ditched the cart and walked out the store. She was right on my heels, still arguing. I noticed Maddie in her car as soon as I walked out the store. We made eye contact before she pulled off. I got in my truck and so did Tiffani.

"I am not going to continue having you disrespect me every time you see that bitch!" Tiffani yelled.

"How did I disrespect you? I didn't even speak to her!" I yelled back.

"You were damn sure looking at her!"

"Are these my eyes or yours? Last I checked, God gave me two eyes to look at what the fuck I want to!" I said.

I was pissed off now. I was sick and tired of this shit. Maybe it was time one of us made the move to get a divorce. I tried, but this shit right here, this was some shit I wasn't going to continue to put up with.

"You are MY HUSBAND… MINE!! That means you are supposed to treat me right!"

"I am your husband, but I'm not your property! You know what? I'm tired of arguing with you. The past three months, I have been doing everything in my power to make this marriage work, but it's not working."

"What are you saying?" she asked.

"I'm saying that maybe it's time we stopped fighting and file for a divorce," I said.

"What?!"

"A divorce!"

"I heard you. I just can't believe you're willing to give up on us so easily," she said as she began to cry. "I'm sorry if I overreacted…"

"OVERREACTED?! You acted like a jealous ass bitch! Do you know how embarrassing that was?"

"I'm sorry, but that doesn't give you the right to call me out my name!"

"I didn't call you a bitch. I said you were acting like one!"

"That's the same as calling me one," she said.

"So now we're going to argue about whether I called you a bitch or not?! This is the shit I'm talking about. You're always looking for a reason to pick a fight with me. I can't go on with this shit!" I said.

"I'm sorry, babe. I just love you so much and I'm so afraid of losing you," she cried.

I didn't bother to answer her because I didn't see a reason to. What would be the point of answering her anyway? She never listens to anything I say. There she sat, crying and boo hooing like a baby, for something that she caused. She caused us to have an argument in front of everybody in that damn store. I was so embarrassed that we didn't even get the groceries that we needed. I pulled up to the front of the house, but I didn't shut the car off.

She turned to look at me as I unlocked the car door. "You're not coming inside?"

"Nah, I got some shit to do."

"Where are you going?" she asked me.

"Does it really matter to you?" I responded.

"Yes, it really does matter."

"I just told you that I have some shit to do! You know, if I were a dog, I would be really mad about the short leash you keep trying to latch around my neck. Stop smothering me, Tiff!"

"Smothering you? Is that what you think I'm doing?"

"Hell yea! Every time I get ready to go somewhere, you're right there with that whining shit! I'm sick of that shit!" I said. "You need to lay off me."

"So, I'm just supposed to sit here while you go fuck your bitch... is that it?" she asked as she continued to cry a river in my fucking truck. I never saw this side of Tiffani before. She used to have this edge about her, this confidence, but now... now, she wasn't even attractive anymore.

The stress was obviously getting to her. She was starting to gain weight and the attitude towards me was on ten. I hadn't seen or touched Maddie since that first night she caught me at Maddie's apartment. Seeing Maddie in the grocery store made me want her even more than before. I tried my best to be a good husband to Tiff, but she wasn't who I wanted anymore.

"I think we should talk about a divorce when I get back," I said softly.

"I don't want a divorce!" she sobbed.

"I think it's for the best, Tiff. You don't need a husband, you need a pet. Go to the pet store and buy a dog. I just can't do this shit no more. Now, if you'll excuse me, I got some place to be." I reached over and opened the door so she could get the hell out of my truck.

She looked at me with tears running all down her face and snot dripping from her nose. That shit was disgusting to me. "I love you, Lincoln. I've never loved a man this much before. I've never fought so hard to make a relationship work like I'm fighting right now. I don't want a divorce. I just want you."

She finally got out the truck and I backed out. She stood in the driveway crying like a kid who just got his favorite toy broken. I couldn't concentrate on her right now. I had to see Maddie. I had to hold her and I had to put my dick inside her. I drove over to her place like a bat outta hell. I couldn't call her first because she had changed her number after that night. We hadn't had any contact whatsoever.

I pulled into the parking lot of her complex and saw her car parked out front. I was instantly excited. Sure, the thought of Tiffani following me here had crossed my mind. I just didn't think after the conversation that we had that she would actually do it. I thought she would take into account what I told her about wanting a divorce and know that I was at my wit's end. I knocked on Maddie's door and rang the doorbell several times before she finally opened it.

She stood there in her bath towel; her shoulders were glistening with water. The shocked expression on her face matched mine when I saw her earlier in the grocery store. She started to ask me why I was here, but I wouldn't let her finish. She already knew why I was here. I made my way into her apartment, closed and locked the door, then took her in my arms. I shoved her against the wall, dropped her towel and my pants, and shoved my pipe inside her. I pumped into her like I was starving for pussy.

For the next couple of hours, we made up for lost time. I heard the doorbell and the beating on the door and we immediately knew who it was. I wasn't going to open that door that easily this time. I had my dick inside Maddie and I wasn't about to stop until I was ready to. I didn't know why my wife insisted on making a fool of herself. That shit had to stop.

She finally stopped pounding on the door and ringing the bell as I continued to slaughter Maddie's sweet tight kitty cat. Speaking of sweet, I had been so busy busting that thang wide open that I forgot to taste it. I pulled out and quickly moved downward until my tongue was deep inside her soft folds. She held on to the sheet as she rode my tongue. Up and down she went as I licked and lapped up her juices like a thirsty dog on a hot summer day. Her moans grew a little louder as she rode to ecstasy. I felt a gush of her sweet nectar and licked up every single drop.

I wiped the excess juices from my chin as I inserted my pole into her again. She cringed and bit down on her bottom lip as I plowed into her with fervor. I couldn't get enough of this woman. It was like I was obsessed with having her. She fulfilled all my needs, wants, and desires when we were together. For a brief second, my unhappy home life flashed before my eyes. I thought how this was the way things were supposed to be with a couple. This was how they were supposed to make each other feel.

I was truly missing out on a lot of good shit by staying with Tiff. Something had to change or I was going to lose my damn mind. I brought my lips down on Maddie's as she opened her mouth to receive my tongue. We kissed like two people who hadn't seen each other in years instead of months. I felt like a soldier returning from my tour and seeing my woman for the first time. I was hungry for her and I could tell that she felt the same way. When I felt my shaft swelling up and the head feeling like it was going to burst, I picked up the pace and plowed deeper inside her.

She screamed in pleasure, "Ooooooouuu! Oh shit! I'm cumming!"

"Cum all over that dick, girl!" I told her.

Her body shook as if she was having a seizure. I felt my own nut find its way to the surface as my toes curled from the intensity. "Awwwww shit!" I cried out.

I pushed my dick as far as it could go as I came inside her. After holding each other for the next couple of minutes, I finally climbed off of her and laid beside her, completely out of breath. She moved closer to me and I happily wrapped my arm around her, kissing her softly on the forehead. No words were exchanged between us as we closed our eyes and fell into a comfortable sleep. I was tired as a muthafucka from that workout, so sleep came real easy for me.

I hadn't planned on spending the night at Maddie's place, but that was what happened.

****

When I woke the next morning, and took in my surroundings. I looked over to my right and Maddie was sound asleep in my arms. She looked like an angel; like she was literally glowing. She was so beautiful and that was when I decided that she was who I wanted to be with. I loved her and she and I should have been married instead of me and Tiff. I made a huge mistake bringing her into my life and making her my wife. I should have never done that shit.

I realized that as long as Maddie would have me, I would never be faithful to Tiffani. That wasn't fair to her and I was going to let her know that the next time I saw her. One day, I hoped that Tiffani could forgive me. I knew that she would be able to find someone who would appreciate her for who she was and all she had to offer. I wasn't that nigga and I hoped that she would understand. I needed a divorce. I wanted a divorce. I wanted to be with Maddie and I didn't want to be tied down to Tiffani anymore. She deserved more than I was willing to give her.

As I wrapped my arm tighter around Maddie, my dick stood at attention. Well, I certainly wasn't going to disappoint him. So, I climbed on top of Maddie and stroked the head of my dick up and down her opening. Once I felt some moisture, I shoved him inside as her eyes popped open. Even though I was invading her space without warning, she picked up her legs and opened them wider for me. She wasted no time throwing that pussy back at me as I shoved my tongue in her mouth, morning breath and all.

Yea, this was where I belonged and I was going to let my wife know as soon as I got home.

Chapter six

Josiah

I had been buried beneath the sheets with my woman ever since I returned from work, but I didn't care. That was exactly where I belonged. She would go to work, come home, and jump right in the bed with me. While she was at work, I busied myself around the house, cleaning and doing a few little repairs that was needed in the apartment. A couple of times, I met up with the fellas for some drinks and to shoot pool.

Smoke always looked like he had something he wanted to tell me, but never did. At a time, I knew that he and Maddie had started messing around because she had confided in Nova and of course, Nova told me. I didn't think that was wise for him to do though. I mean, he was a married man. It wasn't as if he was just playing house with Tiffani. The two of them had stood before a minister and exchanged vows to love each other til death. I couldn't believe my nigga had been sleeping with Maddie.

But, he told me that Tiffani had found out and had confronted him. He said she was so devastated that he had decided to give their marriage another chance. Of course, I wanted him to be happy because he deserved that. He didn't seem happy these past few months though, but lately. Well, let's just say I wondered if he had been hiding something. Especially since he looked happier than I had ever seen him. But, I was his best friend and it wasn't my job to be his conscious. It didn't matter whether I agreed with what he was doing or not, I was still going to support him because it made him happy. I hadn't seen that nigga that happy in months. So, I was going to let him do him and just be happy for him.

Nova had left for work that morning so I decided to clean up the house before hitting my dudes up. I was thinking about firing up the grill and putting some steaks and hamburgers on it. I was going to need to make a quick run to the store though to grab some things I might need. I opened the fridge as I jotted stuff down on my grocery list. Then I went about my business of cleaning the house.

That took a little over two hours. I jumped in the shower and washed all the sweat off me before hopping out and drying myself off. I got dressed and made my way to the bedroom to put some clothes on. I chose a Tommy Hilfiger shirt and a pair of acid washed Levi's relaxed fit jeans. I threw on my retro Jordan's and checked myself out in the mirror.

"You are one helluva good lookin' brotha," I told myself as I ran my fingers along my neatly trimmed goatee. I picked up my Dolce & Gabbana sunglasses, my wallet and truck keys and headed out the door. I was almost to the truck when I realized I had forgotten the shopping list. I ran back inside the house and grabbed it off the counter then headed back out. I was almost to my truck when a car pulled in my driveway.

I looked to see who it was and realized it was Tiffani. I wondered what she was doing here because if she was looking for Smoke, he wasn't here. She stepped out of the car and I could tell she had been crying. She looked like a clown with all that shit running down her face. I was going to have to talk to Smoke about increasing her makeup allowance. She definitely needed the kind that didn't fuck up when she cried. Maybe she came to have a girl chat with Nova, but she was at work.

"Hey Tiff, if you're looking for Nova…"

"I'm not looking for her…"

"Oh, well Smoke ain't here either," I said.

"I'm not looking for his ass either. I already know where he is. I actually wanted to talk to you," she said.

"Me? What do you wanna talk to me about?" I asked. Hell, I was confused as a muthafucka right now. Sure, she and I had spoken before, but mostly just hi and bye. We ain't never had no one on one conversation before so I was definitely wondering why she wanted to talk to me.

"Can we go inside please? I don't want all your neighbors in my business," she said.

"Well, I was actually on my way out."

"I'm sorry, but I really need to talk to you. Please."

Looking at her puppy dog eyes and shit, I shrugged my shoulders and headed inside the house. She followed behind me and I let her in once I had unlocked the door. She stood in the foyer and as soon as I closed the door, she fell into my arms bawling like a baby. I ain't never been in no situation like this before and prayed that Nova would come home early.

I patted her back and waited until she had calmed down. I pushed her out of my arms and asked, "What is this about? Why did you need to talk to me?"

I knew I probably sounded insensitive but I didn't care. This was my best friend's wife and neither he nor my girl were here at that moment, so I needed her to say what she needed to and get to steppin'.

"Smoke is cheating on me. But, I'm sure since the two of you are best friends, you probably already know that," she said.

"Actually, I didn't. I was under the impression that the two of you were working on your marriage."

"Lies! All a bunch of got damn lies!" she fumed. I had never seen her so hurt or angry in my life. Her face was all twisted up and shit so with that bad ass makeup, she looked like she belonged on that movie, *IT*. "I followed him to that bitch, Maddie's house yesterday and he never came home last night! That makes three days that I haven't seen my husband! Three fuckin' days!" she said as she held up three fingers while crying. "I just don't get it. I've been doing everything I can to save my marriage. I cook, I clean, I suck his dick and fuck him, when he lets me anyway. I just don't get it. What's wrong with me, Josiah?"

Oh shit! I was not the one she should be questioning or talking to about her marriage. My loyalty lied with my nigga, Smoke. I didn't know what was going on with him and Maddie because he hadn't spoken to me about it.

"Look, I don't know what's going on between you and Smoke…"

"Didn't you hear anything I said? Nothing is going on between me and Smoke! Absolutely nothing! He's been over at that bitch's house for the past three days!" she cried.

"I haven't seen Smoke since last week. I think if you have an issue with him and what he's doing, you should speak to him. I have nothing to do with you guy's marriage," I said.

"Wow! I guess since he's your best friend, you have to be loyal to him."

"You're right. But, loyalty has nothing to do with this conversation right now. You're married to Smoke, so that's who you should be sharing your feelings and concerns with."

"I tried. I went over there and banged on that door until my knuckles were blue, but they wouldn't open it. I was screaming so loud that the neighbors threatened to call the police, so I left. I'm a good woman. Why would he do me this way?" she cried as she fell into my arms again.

"Please God! Get this woman out of my arms and my house," I silently prayed.

She pulled back from my arms and next thing I knew, she had pressed her lips on mine. I quickly pushed her off me and said, "Yo, this ain't that type of party! You need to speak to your husband."

"I'm so sorry," she said.

"Yea, okay."

"Can I use your restroom before I go?" she asked.

"Yea, down the hall on the left." I pointed.

"I know. This isn't my first time in your house." She walked down the hall and into the bathroom. I went to the sink and washed my face and lips. That woman was definitely trippin'.

I dried my face and hands with the Viva paper towels and waited for her to come out the bathroom. When she emerged from the bathroom in her pink bra and panty set, my mouth hit the floor. She walked seductively over to me as I backed up against the kitchen counter. "You need to put your fuckin' clothes on and get the hell up out my house, Tiff!" I said.

"Please Josiah, don't turn me away. I don't have anyone to turn to and I need you," she said.

"You need something alright, but it definitely ain't me."

She was now rubbing up against me as I stood with my butt against the kitchen counter. I held my hands up to push the fuck out of her, but she grabbed my dick through my pants and said, "You want me. I knew that you did."

"I don't want you, girl! You're my best friend's wife!"

"Your dick says you do want me," she said.

I removed her hands from my package as she smiled wickedly. "You know you want me. Take me, Josiah. It'll be our little secret," she said as she brought her hand back to my dick.

"Fuck no! This shit right here ain't happening so you might as well go get dressed and get out!" I said.

"FINE!" she said as she marched back down the hall angrily. I didn't hear the door close to the bathroom and after five minutes, she still hadn't come out.

I went to look for her because she had to go. As I made my way down the hall, I noticed that the guest room was cracked open. I didn't understand why that was because that door was always closed. "Tiffani, where are you?!" I asked as I looked in the bathroom down the hall. Her clothes were still on the bathroom floor, but she wasn't in there.

I walked across the hall to the guest bedroom and she was lying on the bed, butt ass naked with her legs wide open. Oh my God! What the hell was I going to do now? My dick was jumping angrily behind the zipper of my pants, anxious to be released. I couldn't believe that she was actually doing this. I tried to look away because I really didn't need to see my best friend's wife clitoris or her boobs, but I couldn't tear my gaze away.

"What are you doing, Tiff? Look, I know Smoke hurt you, but this shit here is wrong on so many levels. Now, if you get your clothes, get dressed, and leave. I won't tell him or Nova anything about this. But, if you don't..."

"Josiah, I know you want me because I can see that big monster in your pants. I promise I won't tell," she said. She got on all fours in the bed and crawled to the edge where I was standing. When she reached for my zipper, I grabbed her hand.

"Don't! I'm serious, you need to leave."

"Just let me lick it!" she said as she ran her tongue over her lips. How did I get myself into that situation? Why the hell did I have to be involved in this shit? "I just want somebody to love me, Josiah. Please, just love me."

She started to cry again and that time when she reached for my pants, I didn't stop her. She unzipped them and unbuttoned the button before reaching inside my boxers and pulling out my already hardened shaft. She smiled when she saw the width of it. "Oh my!" she said as she wrapped her lips around it. I gripped her hair as she went to town sucking my meaty pipe.

That shit was amazing! I knew that what we were doing was wrong, so I tried not think about it. I reached under her and played with her clit. She moaned against my dick as she continued to suck it. I inserted two fingers inside her and damn, her shit was so tight. Smoke must not have been hitting it at all. If he was, she wouldn't be that tight. I needed to stop while I was ahead. Things hadn't gotten that far yet between us. I watched as she sucked and stroked my dick. I pulled my fingers from her tight well, but she grabbed them and put them back in. Aw damn!

"Fuck me, Josiah! Fuck me hard!" she begged as she stroked my hard dick and looked me in the eyes. Her eyes were begging me to give it to her. "I need to feel you inside me. Pleeeeaasssseeee!" she continued to beg.

My dick was pulsating in her hands as she continued to stroke it. She smiled at me as she licked my balls and took them in her mouth. Aw shit! That felt so fuckin' good. I dropped my pants to the floor, turned her around, held her ass cheeks open, and plowed into her without another thought. She yelped loudly as I busted that pussy wide open. Her shit was so tight, it wrapped around my dick like a pair of leather gloves. I smacked her ass as she screamed into the down comforter on the bed.

This was what she wanted. She had begged for me to fuck her and that was exactly what I was doing. I wasn't going to take it easy at all. I plowed into her like a jackhammer breaking up concrete on a sidewalk. She continued to scream as I watched my dick go in and out of her with fervor.

SMACK! SMACK! SMACK!

The sounds of our sweaty skin slapping together could probably be heard from outside. I was at a point of no return as I continued to punish her tight pussy. Her pussy was tight and juicy. Her shit was super wet as it made farting noises across the room. "Oh my God! I'm cumming!" she screamed.

A couple seconds later, her body wracked with emotion as she sprayed her cream all over my shaft. I felt my own dick about to cum as I picked up the pace. I was now fucking her so hard that her hair was coming undone. I continued to pummel inside her for a few more minutes until my dick released its own cream. When I was done, I pulled out and said, "Get dressed and get out!"

She looked at me with disappointment all over her face. What the fuck was she expecting me to say after she had seduced me? Did she think I was going to hold her and share a kumbaya moment? I was so ashamed of myself as I picked up my boxers and pants. This shit was so fucking wrong. How could I have been such a damned fool?

"What?" she finally asked.

I walked out and went to the bathroom to get her clothes. I came back in and threw them at her. "GET YO CLOTHES ON, AND GET THE FUCK OUT MY

HOUSE!" I yelled so there wouldn't be any misunderstanding between us. I watched as she hopped out the bed and hurriedly got dressed. She didn't even put her bra and panty back on. She threw her feet in her sandals and rushed to make her exit.

Before she walked out, she turned to me and said, "I'm so sorry." Tears were streaming down her face, but I didn't care.

"Yea, me too. This shit should have never happened!"

She rushed out of the house and to her car. She backed out of the driveway and sped off, like a bat out of hell. I locked my front door and went back to the guest bedroom. I needed to wash the comforter because it had her scent on it. I needed to spray the room with Febreze because it reeked of sex. I pulled the comforter off the bed and made my way to the laundry room. I shoved it in the washing machine and poured the liquid washing powder in, along with some fabric softener. I grabbed the Febreze air freshener and sprayed the room until it smelled like Bora Bora instead of sex.

I made my way back to the bathroom and hopped in the shower, again. I washed myself from head to toe and stepped out once I had rinsed myself off. So much for the plans I had today. The last person I needed to hang with today was Smoke. How the fuck was I going to be able to face my nigga after I had just fucked the shit out of his wife? I dried my body off and applied lotion to my dampened skin. I tossed my clothes in the hamper and took it in the laundry room so I could wash them.

I dressed myself once again and walked through the house, making sure to spray every single corner. I didn't want any traces of Tiffani's ass being in here. My phone began to ring and I knew it was Nova because of the ringtone. She must be on her break. I took a deep breath and answered it, hoping she wouldn't be able to smell the sin from where she was. I had fucked up big time and wondered if I would ever be able to keep this secret.

"Hey baby," I answered.

"Hey you, what you up to?" she asked in her usual cheery voice.

"I was just cleaning up a little."

"Aw babe, thanks. I know the house wasn't that dirty, but the fact that you cleaned up…"

"Girl, stop acting like I never clean up!" I said.

"Well, I didn't say never, but it is a rare moment when you do," she said with a laugh.

"Whatever. Whatchu up to?"

"Nothing much, just missing you."

"I miss you too mama, but you only have a few hours left," I said.

"Yea, I know. I can't wait though," she said.

"Me either."

"Well, I just wanted to touch bases with you and let you know that I'm thinking about you. I love you so much," she gushed on the other end of the phone.

"I love you too, babe. Oh, before I forget… I'm gonna throw some meat on the grill and invite a few friends over. Are you up for entertaining tonight?" I asked.

I didn't want her to walk in and be surprised to see that we had company. If she said no, I'd call Smoke and let him know that we would do the cookout another time. But, she said, "Yea, that's fine. Who are you inviting?"

"Uh, Smoke, Shane and Brian and I'll tell them they can bring their chicks if that's okay with you."

"It's fine. I'll see you when I get home, okay?"

"Yea, okay."

"Smooches," she said as she blew kisses through the phone. We ended the call after that and I continued to clean the house once again. I hated what happened between Tiffani and I. I didn't know how I was going to face Nova and Smoke after what we did. I pulled the comforter out of the washer and stuck it in the dryer. Then I began pulling colored clothes from the hamper and throwing them into the washer. Once I finished with that, I went back into the guest room to make sure that all scents that came from Tiffani was gone.

Confident and satisfied that the room smelled like Febreze, I left the room, closing the door behind me. My phone began to ring so I pulled it from my pocket and saw that Smoke was calling. I didn't want to answer at the moment because Tiffani had just left here about two hours ago, but I knew if I didn't, I'd look suspicious.

"Wassup bro?" I answered, trying my best to sound natural and normal.

"Whatchu doing, ma nigga?" he asked, sounding all cheerful and shit.

"Ah, nothing much. I was cleaning the house a little before Nova came home from work. I was gonna try and put a little meat on the grill…"

"And you wasn't gonna call and invite me, nigga?"

"Yea, I was gonna hit up you, Shane and Brian. I just hadn't had the chance yet. Y'all welcome to bring y'all ol' ladies if y'all want to," I said.

"What time you gonna do that? I'll come early and help you fire shit up!" he said.

"Oh, I guess around six or so. I haven't even gone to the store yet."

"Well, whatchu waiting on?"

"I told you I was cleaning up."

"You want me to bring something?" he asked.

"Some alcohol if y'all wanna drink," I said. "You bringing Tiff?"

I hoped he would say no because I was not trying to see her right now.

"Nah. Is it okay if I bring Maddie?"

Damn! Up until that moment right there, I didn't understand how important Maddie was to Smoke. I knew that Tiffani claimed he hadn't been home in three days, but I figured she was exaggerating. But, by him wanting to invite Maddie to the barbecue, I knew that shit between them was on a whole different level. What nigga would flaunt his side chick around when he had a wife unless he was serious about her?

"Uh, what about your wife?"

"I'll talk to you about that when I get there. Just know I made a decision when it comes to my marriage so Tiff isn't an issue."

"Oh, well aight. See you when you get here," I said before we ended the call.

I went about my business cleaning up before going to the grocery store. This evening was definitely going to be an interesting night...

Chapter seven

Tiffani

When I went over to Nova and Josiah's place, I didn't have any intentions on anything happening between Josiah and myself. But, as I cried on his shoulder, it stirred some feelings in me that I didn't think existed anymore. My husband had been treating me so horribly lately that I thought my feelings had been buried deeper than his love for me. As it turned out, my feelings button worked just fine.

I know it was wrong of me to sleep with my husband's best friend, but hey, what he wouldn't do, another man would, and did. Before I could even have a chance to relax and enjoy the after effects of our "good time," Josiah was throwing me out of his house. I mean, what the hell was wrong with him? One, minute he was all caught up in what we were doing and the next, he was screaming at me like I had threatened to tell Nova. I wouldn't tell Nova about this little episode though.

She was a really sweet person and I wouldn't want to hurt her feelings. I just don't understand how Josiah could treat me that way. It was as if he blamed me for what happened. It wasn't my fault… well, not all my fault. If he really didn't want to, he didn't have to, but he did. And, I could tell from the sounds he was making that he loved it. I couldn't even lie though, his dick was great!

At first, I was shocked that Josiah was speaking to me that way. I knew he was in love with Nova, but we had just shared a moment. When he yelled for me to get the fuck out of his house, I could feel a horrible pain in the pit of my stomach. Why would he say that to me? How could he be so cruel?

I rushed to put my clothes on before he snapped at me again. I put my shoes on and mumbled how sorry I was. Nothing prepared me for his next words. He looked at me and said, "Yea, me too. This shit should have never happened."

Talk about twisting the knife in my gut. I was crying by the time I pulled out of his driveway. Hell, I started crying as soon as he cussed me out. I guess I was just shocked that he had spoken to me that way. I made it home in no time and jumped in the shower. I felt like a dirty whore for sleeping with Josiah. That wasn't even in my character. I was losing myself because of what my husband was doing to me.

I was so upset that once I was done taking my shower, I just curled up under the covers and cried. I almost didn't hear when my husband finally came home. He walked in the bedroom and went straight to the bathroom. I heard the shower running and fifteen minutes later, he came out. I heard him rummaging through the dresser drawers and figured he was getting dressed to leave again.

Finally, I guess he noticed me under the covers. He shook me gently and sat on the side of the bed. "Aye, you aight?" he asked.

Wow! He was acting like he really gave a shit how I felt.

He nudged me again and said, "I'm talking to you, guh."

I peeked out from under the covers, sure that my eyes and nose were red from crying. He looked at me and asked, "What's the matter witchu?"

"Like you care," I said sarcastically.

"I wouldn't have asked if I didn't care."

"You don't think I should feel some kind of way about you sleeping with that girl? I mean, you're doing it out in public and not giving two shits about how I feel," I cried. Of course, the incident with Josiah had me feeling some kind of way too, but this mostly had to do with my husband.

"Look, I'm sorry about that. I-I-I-I, hell, I don't even know what else I can say. I didn't mean for shit to happen like that."

"We're married, Lincoln!" I said as I flashed my wedding set in his face. I looked at his left hand and he still was wearing his wedding band. Just that sign made me think that maybe we still had a chance. "Can I ask you something?"

He rolled his eyes, but said, "Yea, go ahead."

"Why did you marry me?"

"What?"

"You heard me… why did you marry me?"

He waited a couple of minutes before he responded. "I married you because I loved you."

"Loved? So, you don't love me anymore?" I asked as the tears threatened to fall again. I was so sick of crying over a man.

"I still love you, Tiff. I think I'll always love you," he said.

"Okay, so let me see if I got this straight. You married me because you love me. You still love me, and you think you will always love me. Am I missing something?" I asked. My husband was sitting next to me without a shirt, in only his boxer briefs. I stared at his dick for a minute because he just smelled so good. I was a woman who was deeply in love with my husband, so seeing him and inhaling his scent had my clit throbbing.

"What are you talking about?"

"I mean, if you love me, why aren't we together? Why are you cheating on me if you love me?"

"Because…"

He just let the word dangle there and looked down at the comforter. He needed to finish that sentence. I needed to know what he wanted to say. "Because what, Lincoln?"

"I don't want to say anything that'll hurt your feelings."

I swallowed the lump in my throat and wondered what he was going to say to hurt my feelings. I mean, he had already hurt me. Could whatever he had to say hurt me any more than he already had?

"Just say it," I said as I braced myself.

"I love you, but I'm not in love with you. I never was," he said softly.

He was right, that shit did hurt. It cut me so deep that the tears that were threatening to fall couldn't be held back anymore. "See? That's why I didn't wanna say anything," he said. "I'm really sorry, Tiff. I never meant to hurt you."

I just continued to sob uncontrollably. I felt that shit in my heart just as if he had punched me in the stomach. That was how bad it hurt. He wrapped his arms around me and held me while I cried on his shoulder. I held my husband tight and close to me, inhaling his musky and Gio scents. I always loved the way he smelled. I let the covers drop from my top half, so now we were skin to skin. I wasn't sure if he felt the same flames I did, but I was going to take advantage of this moment.

I pulled away and looked him in the eyes. "What am I supposed to do?"

"I'm not sure. Now is not the time to talk about that. We'll figure things out one day," he said.

"But, I-I-I love you s-s-s-s-so much," I cried and gasped for air at the same time. I couldn't believe he had said he never was in love with me. I swear, men knew just what to say to twist the knife that they implanted in a woman's heart. I was his wife. Didn't that mean anything to him anymore?

"I care a lot about you, Tiff."

"Just not enough to stay with me," I said sadly.

"My heart belongs to someone else," he said.

"Are you in love with her?" I asked. Then, before he could answer, I decided I didn't really want to know the answer to that question. "Never mind. I don't wanna know."

I started crying again. This time when he put his arms around me to comfort me, I kissed him. Not a peck on the lips, but I drove my tongue down his throat like I needed his air to breathe. At first, he resisted, but it wasn't long before he began to respond. As my hand crept to his boxer briefs, I felt the dick I had come to love grow. I stroked and rubbed it as it came to life.

He shook his head from side to side as he tried to push me away, but I wasn't about to let that happen. I immediately crawled onto his lap and stuck my titty in his mouth. As I grinded on his meat pole and he sucked on my breast, I reached in his briefs and pulled his dick out. He moaned as I stroked it before sliding my wet pussy onto it. He gasped as I contracted the muscles of my sugar walls to latch on to his dick. I rode his dick like a cowgirl at a rodeo. He lay back on the bed and gripped my hips. I met every one of his thrusts with a bounce and ride.

"Oh my God! That's it baby, fuck me!" I cried as I placed my hands on his chest and bucked harder. He was hitting my G-spot so hard, my insides cringed. I could feel my orgasm ready to burst as I bounced up and down on his big dick.

People might think I was a hoe for sleeping with my husband and his best friend in the same day, but it wasn't as if I planned it. I loved my husband so as far as I was concerned, what happened between Josiah and I never happened. "Mmmmm!" Lincoln moaned as he sat up.

He buried his head in my chest and sucked my breasts like a newborn starving for his mama's milk. "Oh shit! I'm cummmming!" I cried as I creamed on his dick.

He squeezed my ass cheeks and stood up from the bed. As he gripped my cheeks and I held onto his neck, he bounced my ass up and down on his dick as he stood in the middle of the bedroom. I watched as he plowed into me from the dresser mirror. He kept his head down, almost as if he didn't want to see what we were doing. I didn't care. The fact that we were making love after all this time made me believe we still had a chance to save our marriage.

Our room smelled of sex and sweat. I inhaled the scent as he continued to drive deeper inside me. He pressed my back against the wall and fucked me like a wild animal. I moaned and screamed loud. I wanted my neighbors to hear us having sex. I wanted them to know that my husband was here to stay.

I contracted my muscles again and he cried, "Aahhh shit! FUCK!"

He began to slay my pussy like a hair dresser with a hot comb. I held on for dear life as he drove his dick inside me like a jackhammer. "Damn! That's some good pussy!" he said against my chest. "Mmmm! Maddie!"

I pretended like I didn't hear him call me by that homewrecker's name as he continued to punish my kitty. I loved my husband so much, but the tears flowed from my eyes. I tried to fight them, but I couldn't. I was so devastated. I continued to hold on as he went in and out with fervor. Twenty minutes later, he succumbed to his orgasm and bursts inside me. He thrusted once more and held me tight. Finally, after several minutes, he lowered me to the floor and stuffed his dick in his briefs.

He looked away from me as if he was ashamed that we had just had sex. He wouldn't even look me in the eyes, probably embarrassed that he had called me by her name. He walked into the bathroom and closed the door. I could hear the water to the shower get turned on. I laid in the bed feeling like shit. My pussy was still throbbing from the beat down he just gave it, but my heart was completely shattered by what I heard. I couldn't contain my emotions as I broke down the way I had earlier that day.

Lincoln exited the bathroom a few minutes later and began to put some clothes on. I dried my tears and asked, "Where are you going?"

"Out," was all he said.

"Where?"

"Uh, I think we established that I have one mother and her name ain't Tiffani," he said as he side eyed me.

"I don't want to be your mom, but I am your wife. Where are you going, Lincoln? We need to talk about what just happened?" I cried.

"What's to talk about? You was hot. You wanted some dick so I gave it to you. That don't change the fact that I still ain't in love witchu," he said.

Tears threatened to fall, but I wouldn't let them. Why did he make love to me just now if we weren't getting back together? "But, we just made love," I countered.

"Who just made love?" he asked with a smirk on his face.

"Don't do me, Lincoln! WE, YOU AND ME. WE JUST MADE LOVE!"

"The hell! We, you and me, we just fucked… nothing more, nothing less. Just two people fucking for a good time!" he corrected me.

"How can you talk to me like that? Like…"

"Like what?"

"Like some trick on the street!"

"I'm just being honest. Do you want me to lie to you?" he asked.

I didn't know how to answer that question. If I said yes, he would lie to me. If I said no, he wouldn't tell me anything. I didn't know what to say.

"But, why are you leaving? Why can't you just stay home so we could spend some time together?"

"I got plans, that's why."

"Can I come?" I asked.

"Come where?"

"With you," I said with a hopeful smile.

"Nah, I'm good."

"Wow! Okay, do you then, Lincoln! Just don't expect me to be sitting around here waiting when you decide you made a mistake!" I said.

I was literally crushed by his attitude. I cared so much about this man and he had tossed me aside like some trick. I felt worse than I did before so I just sunk back under my covers and hoped that sleep would come soon. I didn't want to have to think about nothing else today, especially not my husband or his best friend. Wherever he was going, he sure didn't want me there.

Chapter eight

Nova

I got home from work to find the house clean and smelling so good. I was glad that my man had cleaned up. He was always so helpful around the house. I saw his truck in the driveway so I knew he was home. I went to the bedroom in search of him and heard the shower running. I could definitely use a little steam fresh loving so I dropped my bag on the bench at the foot of the bed, took off my shoes, and made my way towards the bathroom.

I undressed and slid the shower door open. He turned around when he heard the door open and smiled when he saw me step in. I moved over to him and kissed him softly on the lips. The kiss grew deeper as I slipped my tongue into his mouth and mine began to do the tango with his. I reached down and began to stroke his dick. It was semi hard and usually jumped to my touch, but today, it wasn't responding. I continued to stroke it as we kissed, but after several minutes, it still wasn't hard.

I could tell he was becoming uncomfortable so I stopped. He rinsed himself off and got out. I didn't understand what was going on or why he didn't get up the way he usually did. I figured he needed a little time to himself, so when he stepped out, I stayed behind to finish washing me. By the time I was done, Josiah had left the bedroom. I guess he was embarrassed by what happened in the shower. He had no reason to be embarrassed; shit happened. That was the first time that happened to him with me, but he still shouldn't be embarrassed by it.

I knew he had thrown this little get together at the last minute so maybe he was stressing about it. Usually, when we decided to have gatherings, I was also off so we could work together. I heard the doorbell ringing so I knew that some of our guests had arrived. I quickly slipped into a maxi dress and a pair of sandals. I put on some deodorant and perfume before joining the gang.

While Brian and Josiah went outside to man the grill, Tammy and I adjourned to the kitchen to start the side dishes. Tammy was Brian's girlfriend of two years. She and I had spent some time together before at other cookouts and when we all got together for date night. She was nice and loved Brian so much. She was patiently waiting for him to ask her to marry him, but for some reason, he was holding back.

As we sat down to peel the potatoes, the doorbell chimed again. I stood up to get it and was surprised to see Maddie and Smoke together. I mean, he was still married and I thought she understood that. She was crossing a boundary that was sure to get her hurt. Why do women chase after married men anyway? That man wasn't going to leave his wife for Maddie and I wished she would understand that.

"Hey BFF!" Maddie greeted me as she reached for a hug.

I hugged my best friend, but we were going to have to talk later. I still carried some guilt over the fact that I had ratted her and Smoke out to his wife. I just didn't think that the two of them should have been carrying on that way knowing that he had a wife at home. They should have gotten together before he got married, not now. "Hey girl, I didn't know you were coming," I said.

"Oh, Josiah didn't tell you that I was bringing Maddie?" Smoke asked.

"No, when he mentioned you were coming, I assumed you would be bringing Tiffani. That's why I didn't bother to invite Maddie because I was trying to keep the drama to a minimum," I said. "Y'all come on in."

I stepped to the side and they walked in. "The guys are in the backyard and Tammy and I were cutting potatoes for the potato salad."

Smoke kissed Maddie on the temple before disappearing through the double doors that led to the backyard. "Do I sense some hostility directed towards me?" Maddie asked.

"No, I just don't want you to get hurt by Smoke again. I mean, he still has a wife, Maddie."

"I know that, but he doesn't love her. He's going to ask her for a divorce," she said, sounding confident.

"And you think she's just going to give it to him?"

"I don't know, but I hope now that she knows about us, she will. He doesn't love her, Nova. He loves me and I love him too." The smile on her face could light up a room. I could tell that she believed everything that Smoke had told her. I wanted to be happy for her, but something told me that Tiffani wasn't going to just let things go that easily.

"C'mon, let's go help Tammy before she decides to leave," I said as I linked my arm through hers. We headed to the kitchen to help Tammy.

****

Later that evening, as Josiah and I lay in bed, I could tell that he was tense. I wondered what was bothering him so I decided to ask him. Josiah and I had never kept secrets from each other so if something was on his mind, I needed him to know that he could talk to me about it.

"Babe."

"Yea."

"Is something wrong?" I asked.

"Whaddya mean?"

"I mean, you've been tense ever since the shower earlier," I said.

He didn't respond at first and as I propped myself up on my elbow, I could tell that something was weighing heavily on his mind. "I'm sorry about that. I really am," he said. "Nothing like that has ever happened to me before."

"I know. But, is something wrong? You seem to have something on your mind. You know you can talk to me about anything, right?"

He inhaled deeply and exhaled. "Yea, I know. Nothing's bothering me. I don't know why that shit happened."

"Baby, I love you and even if you're having a bad day, I still love you. Now, if you want to I can try something else to get him up," I smiled as I ran my fingers along his stomach.

"You really want some dick tonight, huh?" he smiled.

"Whatchu think? I worked hard today. I deserve some dick," I said.

I kissed him passionately as he moaned. My kisses trailed along his chest to his belly and finally, to the man of the hour. I stroked it as I took it in my mouth. It wasn't long before his manhood was standing strong and tall. I wasted no time straddling my man. As he pumped into me, I bucked on top of him. Oh my God! His dick felt so good inside me. This was just what I needed after a long day at work and then coming home to entertain our friends.

Josiah gripped my ass cheeks and slammed his dick into my kitty. I could feel that shit in my stomach as he drove me to orgasmic pleasures I had never reached before. We continued our romp in the bed for the next couple of hours. By the time we finished we were out of breath, sweaty, and happy. As he wrapped me in his arms, I closed my eyes and fell asleep instantly. I was pooped.

****

Three months later...

For the past two months, I had been feeling sick to my stomach. At first, I thought it was a virus, but it wouldn't let up. I vomited morning, noon, and night. I just couldn't understand what was going on with me. It wasn't until I had a conversation with my mom that she had me thinking I might be pregnant. That thought had never crossed my mind once. Josiah and I had always been really careful when having sex. And then it dawned on me that we weren't so careful the night of the get together. That was the day he couldn't get it up, but that night, he performed like a champ.

It hadn't occurred to me that not putting a condom on that night could get me knocked up. I called Maddie up and asked her would she come with me to the doctor. I would have asked Josiah, but he was offshore.

"Is everything alright?" she asked, concern dripping from her voice.

"Well, you know I haven't been feeling good lately. My mom just put it in my head that I might be pregnant, so I made a doctor's appointment. Will you come with me?" I asked.

"When is your appointment?"

"Day after tomorrow at one. Can you make it?"

"Yea, sure. I'll go with you," she said.

"Thanks Maddie. You're always there when I need you."

"That's what best friends are for."

As soon as she said that, the betrayal I bestowed on her washed over me and so did the guilt. I didn't know how I could ever forgive myself for that, but I knew there was no way I was ever going to tell her I played a part in Tiffani finding out about her and Smoke's affair. That was one secret I would be taking to the grave.

"Yea, you're right. I'll see you in a couple of days and thanks again," I said.

"Will you stop thanking me? I'll always look out for you and I'm not doing anything for you that you wouldn't do for me."

"You're right," I said. We ended the call shortly thereafter, with me feeling like the most disloyal friend ever. After all that Maddie and I had been through, I couldn't believe I had did her like that.

****

Two days later, Maddie and I sat in the waiting room at the doctor's office. When my name was called, I stood up and we walked to the back. I was weighed, then had my temperature, blood pressure, and pulse checked. "What brings you here today?" the nurse asked.

"I think I might be pregnant," I said.

"What are your symptoms and when was your last cycle?" she asked.

"Um, I've been vomiting and feeling a little lightheaded."

"How long has this been going on?"

"A couple of months," I said.

"Do you remember when your last cycle was?"

"I think I had one last month… I don't know," I said as I tried to recall when my last period was.

"Well, it's okay. Let me get a urine sample and then we'll put you in a room and come draw your blood," the nurse named Reva said. She handed me a little plastic cup with a lid and a small package. I turned the package over in my hand trying to figure out what it was. "Oh, I need you to use that to wipe your bottom first. Then pee in the cup and you don't need to fill it all the way. When you're done, you'll see the small window. Place the cup on the wooden sill and knock on the little door. The lab tech will retrieve the cup to run the test."

I went into the small restroom and did as she asked. When I was done, I washed my hands and walked out. I was led to exam room three where Maddie was waiting for me. "You okay?"

"Duh! I just peed in a cup, girl!" I said as we laughed.

"I know, but I'm just making sure."

I smiled at her, even though the smile didn't quite reach my eyes. As we sat and waited for the doctor, my legs shook because I was so nervous. I didn't know what a pregnancy would mean for me and Josiah's relationship. We hadn't talked about having kids before. I didn't even know how he would feel about having a baby with me. I loved him so much. I just hoped that the two of us could stay together for the sake of our child if I was pregnant.

There was a soft knock on the door and the nurse walked in with a dude in a white coat. "Hey Nova, this is Jamison. He's going to draw your blood," said Reva.

"I was hoping y'all wouldn't have to do that," I said.

Reva smiled and Jamison said, "It won't be that bad. The needle is really small. It'll probably feel like a mosquito bite."

I hoped that was how it felt. I literally hated needles and getting stuck with them. Jamison was right though; it didn't hurt that much. It was like a pinch and before I knew it, he was packing his stuff up and leaving the room. Reva said, "We'll be back in a bit with your results."

"Are you nervous?" Maddie asked.

"A little. Josiah and I have never talked about having kids, so I don't know how he's going to feel about that," I said.

"Josiah loves you. He's going to be happy to have a baby with you," she said with a smile. I felt good about that for a minute. Josiah did love me and in that moment, I thought that we would be fine.

Five minutes later, there was another knock on the door. "Hello, Nova," Doctor Sanford greeted me as she and Reva walked in. Doctor Sanford had been my doctor for as long as I could remember. She was the only doctor I trusted with my life.

"Hi, Doctor Sanford," I greeted her with a smile.

"Hello, Madison. Long time, no see," Doctor Sanford greeted Maddie.

"Hey, Doctor Sanford. When I'm feeling good, I don't see a need to come by and bother you," Maddie said.

"Um hmm! So, Reva tells me that you think you're pregnant," she said.

"Well, I think I have all the symptoms, but I'm not sure. That's why I came to see you," I stated.

"Well, you were right to come see me. As it turns out, you are pregnant! Congratulations!" Doctor Sanford said.

"Congrats, girl!" Maddie said from the chair across from me. She was smiling brighter than a cat that swallowed the canary.

I just sat there stunned. I couldn't believe that I was going to be a mother. My hand instantly went to my stomach as I rubbed the area where my baby would be housed for the next few months. "How do you feel?" Doctor Sanford asked.

"I'm going to be someone's mommy," I said as tears rained down my cheeks.

"Yes, you are," Doctor Sanford said.

"Um, how far is she?" Maddie asked.

"I'm not sure. She might be a couple of months. We'll know for sure once she has an ultrasound. But, for now, let's just say since she started getting sick two months ago, she should be around eight to nine weeks along. I can refer you to one of my colleagues who is an OB/GYN. She's really good and we've been friends for a long time," Doctor Sanford said.

"Okay," I said.

"I'll have Celeste make the appointment for you and she'll call you with the details. I'll have her request the earliest available."

"Thank you, Doctor Sanford," I said as Maddie and I stood up. "Bring this chart with you and give it to Celeste. Good luck with your pregnancy!" Doctor Sanford gave me a hug and gave Maddie a stern look. "As for you, young lady, I'll be expecting you to make an appointment for a check-up real soon. Do you understand?"

"I'm not sick," Maddie said.

"You don't come to see the doctor just when you're sick. You're supposed to see your doctor once every six months to make sure you don't get sick," Doctor Sanford advised.

"Okay," Maddie simply responded.

We left the exam room and took the file to Celeste. "Congratulations on your pregnancy! Doctor Sanford wants me to contact Doctor Russo to make your appointment. I'll call the office and make the appointment for you and I'll give you a call with the details."

"Okay, thank you," I said.

We left the office and walked to the car. As I slid in the seat and Maddie did the same, I was in total shock. I was excited and scared at the same time. I couldn't wait to share the news with Josiah. At this point, I was going to hope his reaction was a happy one.

Chapter nine

Maddie

Things between Lincoln and I had been perfect over the past couple of months. Last week, he finally decided to move in with me and I couldn't be happier. I finally got to be with the man I loved and not have to worry about him going back to Tiffani. I would be lying if I said that I didn't feel bad for her, but it wasn't my fault her man wanted me. If Lincoln had never pursued me, we wouldn't be together now. So, I guess that old saying is true… 'If you keep your man happy at home, he has no reason to seek someone else'. The same went for a woman and keeping her happy. And oh my God! Lincoln had been keeping me super happy.

After I went with Nova to the doctor the other day, it made me feel like if she could be that happy, so could I. Now that we both had men of our own, maybe it was time for us to do all we could to keep them. Nova was having a baby, but I wasn't ready for all that yet. I was too wrapped up in my man to even think about sharing him with someone else. He had filed for divorce from Tiffani, citing irreconcilable differences before he left for work. I wondered if she had been served with the papers yet.

The apartment that I was living in was big enough for the two of us, so it was easy for him to move right on in. My bedroom was spacious and had a huge walk-in closet, which I was more than happy to share with him. He hadn't brought too much stuff when he moved in, but he said once he came back from work, he would get all his stuff to make it permanent.

I was so excited and in love. For once in my life, I was truly happy. I hadn't felt this happy since before my dad was killed. Lincoln and I had been spending so much time together, making love, going out, making love, and just being happy. He had been offshore for two and a half weeks and I missed him. We talked and texted every day though, so it made my longing for him not as bad as if we had no communication.

I was getting ready for work one afternoon when I heard the doorbell. I looked at my watch and saw that it was almost one thirty. I wasn't sure who it was, but whoever it was needed to go away. I continued to get ready for work because I had to be there by three.

DING DONG! DING DONG!

I could tell the person wasn't just going to leave me alone, so I had no choice but to answer it. I went to the door and pulled it back to find Tiffani standing on the other side. I plastered a fake smile on my face, wondering why she was here. I had no reason to dislike the woman because technically, she didn't do me anything. I was the one who took her husband away from her, but I still wanted to know why she was on my doorstep.

"Lincoln isn't here, he's at work," I informed her.

"Don't you think I know my husband's work schedule?" she asked with a smirk on her face.

"So, if you know he isn't here, why are you?" I asked, as I smirked right back at her.

"I came to see you. May I come in?"

I didn't really want her in my apartment. It was where I rested my head and lived my happy life with her soon to be ex-husband. But, I remembered the last time I left her outside and the ruckus she caused; all the shouting to let my neighbors know that I was having an affair with Lincoln. I stepped to the side and allowed her entry because I was not looking for a repeat of those nights.

"Say what you need to say and leave. I have to get to work soon." I stated.

"You're so confident in yourself and seem proud of the fact that you stole my husband. I mean, you literally stole my husband and I never suspected you. You were helping me at the hospital when I had my miscarriage. You saw how broken I was when I lost our baby and yet, you still saw fit to steal my husband from me," she said as tears brimmed from her eyes.

"I'm sorry if you got hurt…"

"IF I GOT HURT?! Of course, I'm hurt. He was my husband for two years before you came along and shook your little tail feather in his face," she said.

"That wasn't how it happened. He pursued me. When I found out that he was married, I tried to stay away from him. But, he continued to pursue me. He said he wasn't happy with you and the marriage…"

"So, instead of telling him to seek counseling, you decided to fuck him!"

"Excuse you! It isn't my job to tell your husband how to save a marriage he wasn't interested in saving. I know you don't want to hear this, but if you had kept him happy at home, he wouldn't have sought me out so badly," I said.

WHAP!

That bitch had the nerve to slap me across the face.

WHAP!

I slapped her bitch ass right back. I wasn't interested in getting into a fight in my place, but if that was what she wanted, I would give it to her. She held her cheek with her mouth open, apparently shocked that I had struck her back. "Don't you ever touch me again!" I said through clenched teeth as I pointed my finger. "If I call the police on your ass, you will be arrested. I have the right to fuck you up and get you arrested because you're in my apartment. I'm not going to do that, though, because I understand that you're hurt. I'm sorry that Lincoln doesn't love you anymore. I'm sorry your marriage is over, but I won't apologize for him wanting to be with me. I love him and he loves me. He did file for divorce, ya know?" I asked with a smirk. I was sure that she had gotten served by now, but the look on her face told me that she hadn't.

Her mouth opened, kinda like her jaw hit the floor. She looked so hurt as the tears rained down her face. I didn't have any other words for her. After a couple of minutes of crying and just staring at me, she finally spoke. "He filed for divorce?"

"I'm sorry, I thought you had been served." I said. I really was sorry that I had blurted it out. I just thought she had been served with the papers already. I didn't want to be the one to break the news to her.

"I won't let you have my husband! You can't have him! I love him!" she cried through her tears.

"He doesn't love you and he's already mine," I said.

I didn't want to hurt her feelings that way, but she left me no choice. I had to get her to see that she was wasting her time chasing after him when he didn't want to be caught. "You think you're so smart. You think you've won, huh? Okay, we'll see who has the last laugh, bitch!" she said. "I will never give my husband a divorce. We married for better or worse, so if you thought it was going to be that easy for you to have him, think again!"

"Get out of my apartment please. I have shit to do!" I said as I walked towards the door.

I opened the door and turned to find her still rooted in the same spot. "You have five seconds to get the hell out of my place before I call the cops and have you arrested for trespassing!" I said through clenched teeth as I narrowed my eyes at her.

She finally walked towards me and smiled as she got close to me. "You will never have my husband, bitch!"

"I already have him and he won't be your husband for long. Now, get the fuck out!" I said.

She looked at me with disgust written all over her face. I didn't give a shit how disgusted she was with me. I said I was sorry, so what else was she looking for from me. I wasn't going to keep apologizing when this was Lincoln's decision. He wanted me. He pursued me. She finally walked out and I slammed my door behind her. "Stupid bitch!"

****

Ten days later...

I had taken the day off today because my man was coming home. I couldn't wait to see him either. I had cooked a meatloaf with some mashed potatoes and gravy, some whole kernel corn and baby carrots and Pillsbury crescent rolls. I couldn't wait for him to get here so I could shower him with kisses and pussy.

Josiah was supposed to drop him off when they got back, so all I had to do was wait. He texted me when they got off the boat.

Lincoln: Aye babe, we just got on the road. Gimme a couple hours

Me: Ok, I can't wait to see u

Lincoln: Ditto babe. My dick is hard already. Send me a pic

He was so nasty, but I had no problem sending my man a pic of all he was about to get. I went into the bathroom, stripped down to my birthday suit and climbed on the counter. I posed seductively as I spread my legs. I snapped the pic and satisfied with what I saw, I hit the send button.

Lincoln: I just slapped Josiah so he could push this truck faster...LOL!!

Me: Careful, you gon' make that boy wreck! LOL!!

Lincoln: I'll be there soon. I love you

Me: I love you too, babe

I pressed my phone to my chest with a huge smile on my face. My kitty began to throb just thinking about seeing my man. I heard the oven timer go off, so I hopped off the counter and threw my robe on. I ran to the kitchen to check my meatloaf. The last thing I needed was to serve my man burnt meatloaf after a two-hour ride home. I pulled the meatloaf out of the oven and took the foil off the top of the pan. Then, I put it back in the oven for a few more minutes. I took the potatoes out of the pot and mashed them, as well as made the gravy.

I had cooked the carrots and corn thirty minutes ago, so I prepared to put the crescent rolls in the oven when the meatloaf was done. Thirty minutes later, my meal was perfect. Thirty minutes after that, I heard a vehicle pull into the front of our apartment. I peeked in the window and saw my man getting his things out of the back of the truck. I ran to the bathroom, dropped the robe I had on, and sat my naked ass back on the counter. I wanted to have myself in the same position I was in when I took the pic earlier.

I heard the front door open and Lincoln calling my name. "Maddie! Babyyy!"

"I'm in the bathroom, babe!" I called back.

"Whatchu…" he was asking as he walked in and saw me. "Well damn!" He moved over to where I was sitting and stepped between my open legs. He began to feel me up and kiss me as we worked at taking off his clothes. I unzipped his pants and unbuttoned them. They dropped to the floor with a thud and he tossed his shirt to the side.

His kisses trailed to my belly until he found the treasures he was looking for. "Mmmm!" he said as he got to munching on my cookies. I wrapped my legs around his head as I bucked my kitty in his mouth. It had been 28 long days since I had last been pleasured by my man.

"Ouuu!" I moaned. "Oh God! Yaaaassssss! Right there!"

He definitely knew what he was doing when it came to eating pussy. This man could give a class to those who didn't know what the hell they were doing. My body shook as I exploded in his mouth. He slurped and sucked my juices before standing up and kissing me. I licked and kissed all my cream off his face.

It didn't take long for his dick to find entrance into my love tunnel. As he lifted me off the counter, he stood in the middle of the bathroom floor, gliding my pussy onto his thick, meaty shaft. "Ohhhhhhh God! That feels sooooo good!" I cried as he continued to hit my G-spot.

"I missed you!" he said in a breathless tone.

"I missed you," I said.

"Oh shit! That pussy feels so good!"

"Mmmm hmm!" I said.

My pussy had busted in an orgasm at least four times. I held on to my man as he moaned loud in my ear. "Ssshhitt!" he growled as his semen sprayed my insides. I just held onto him as we kissed passionately. His dick had yet to slip out of me, even though it wasn't as hard as it just was.

Finally, he let me down and said, "Now, that's how you welcome your man home." He bent his head to kiss me again and grabbed my butt. "C'mon and take a shower with me."

"You know if we get in this shower…"

"C'mon girl," he said as he dragged me by my hand. He didn't even wait for the water to get hot. He turned it on and pulled me in. I shrieked at the feel of the cold water on my hot flesh. As the water rained down on us, he turned me around to face the wall and drove his dick inside me from behind.

I moaned as he pressed me against the shower wall and rubbed my clit with his fingers. I was in absolute pleasure mode as he drove me to ecstasy. I had never felt this way about a man before. I bit down on my lip as he nibbled on my back. This was too much. He was doing too much to pleasure me. He was hitting it from the back while he played with my clit and nibbled on my back and shoulder. Good God! I loved when he came back home because he was insatiable.

Our lovemaking session in the shower lasted until the warm water ran out. The cool water sprayed us as we continued to get it in. When we finally succumbed to the emotions inside us, we were totally spent and breathless. We finally were able to keep our hands to ourselves long enough to scrub our bodies. I stepped out of the shower, barely able to walk. My legs felt like Jell-O from the dick down my man had just given me.

"What smells so good?" he asked.

"It's your favorite; meatloaf and mashed potatoes."

"Mmmmm! Thank you, baby!" he kissed me in appreciation. We dried ourselves off and made our way to the bedroom. We threw on some clothes and headed to the kitchen. I fixed us each a plate while he poured us some sweet tea. We sat at the bar to eat.

"Tiffani came by to see me," I said.

"Huh? What'd she come see you for?"

"She wanted me to know that she wasn't giving up on y'all's marriage and how she thought I was a bitch."

"I'm sorry, baby," he said as he rubbed my thigh. "She shouldn't have come here. I'll talk to her about it when I go over there to get the rest of my clothes tomorrow."

"Okay. Babe, why do you think she thinks she can salvage y'all's marriage?" I asked.

"I don't know. I ain't been giving her any indication that I wanted to be with her anymore. I told her that I loved you and I even moved from there in here with you. I don't want Tiff no more. I love you, baby."

"I love you too, honey." I leaned over and kissed him.

I stuck my tongue inside his mouth and he said, "You better stop it now. You gon' start something and we ain't gon' never finish eating."

"You're right!" We both laughed hard.

Who would have known that the next day, he would come back home from visiting Tiffani and my world would come crashing down around me.

****

"She's pregnant." Those two words almost gave me a heart attack. Tiffani was pregnant? If she was pregnant, it wasn't his. Why was he acting this way when I knew that baby wasn't his?

"How? How can she be pregnant?"

He looked at me as if I had just asked the dumbest question in the world. "Do you really want me to answer that?"

"Yes, I do. Especially since the two of you weren't even supposed to be fucking anymore!" I yelled.

I was filled with mixed emotions. I wanted to cry, but I wanted to slap him and punch him. I loved him, but I wanted to hurt him for hurting me and ruining our plans for happiness. Why would he do that to me? Why the hell would he do that to us?

He looked at me as he struggled with his words. "I never told you that we weren't having sex. I mean, she is my wife. What could I do?" he asked, as he shrugged his shoulders.

Now, I was bawling like a baby. We were finally living together after fifteen months of sneaking around. After fifteen months of promises and lies, we had finally beat the odds and proved everyone wrong. He was finally getting a divorce and we were finally going to be married. We hadn't gotten engaged yet, but I knew it was only a matter of time. But, now that his wife was pregnant, I didn't know what would happen to us. Why did God hate me so much? Why would he give me my man and this little taste of happiness if he was only going to strip it away from me?

"I'm sorry, baby. I never meant for this to happen. We didn't even think that she could get pregnant. We had been trying for years and nothing happened. I didn't think that she would get pregnant after all this time."

"But, I love you. What am I supposed to do if you go back to her?" I cried. "What's gonna happen to me? What about our plans for our future?"

"I'm sorry." I wished he would stop saying that shit. Sorry… what the fuck was I supposed to do with a damn sorry? "I wish things had turned out differently, but I have to go back to my wife."

"NO Lincoln! You can't! You promised me that we would be happy! You promised me that you wouldn't leave me again!" I cried.

"This isn't my fault and I meant everything I said to you! I don't wanna leave you, I love you. But, I don't have a choice. My wife is pregnant and she needs me. I can't let her go through this pregnancy by herself. What kind of man would that make me?" Lincoln asked.

"How far along is she?" I asked as I continued to sob like a little kid.

"Ten weeks."

Ten weeks? I expected him to say at least four, five, even six months. But, they were still sleeping together ten weeks ago. I started crying again. When he made the move to get past me, I didn't stop him that time. But, I couldn't let him go. I loved him too much. I jumped up from the floor where I had sunk and rushed after him.

"WAIT, LINCOLN!" I bounded out the door after him as he was placing his duffle bag in the trunk. He turned to look at me and I said, "You can't leave me!"

"I already explained…"

"But, I'm pregnant too!" I blurted out. I hadn't even thought about what I was going to say before I said it. I just couldn't lose him, so I just said whatever I thought I needed to say to keep him from leaving me. After everything we had been through, I couldn't let him go without a fight. It just seemed like the only thing I could say to keep my man. Telling him that I was pregnant too was something that I was going to have to handle… in time.

"What?" he asked as he stood there looking at me.

"I'm pregnant."

"How? When?"

"I think you know how and when was about eleven weeks ago," I said. My heart was beating so fast and so loud, I just knew he would recognize that I was lying.

"When did you find this out?" he asked with a confused look on his face.

"I just found out a few days ago. I was going to tell you over a romantic dinner, but then you came with some news of your own." I said. "Don't you see? This can only be the work of the Lord. We belong together. We're gonna be a family, baby." I placed his hand on my belly and looked into his eyes.

His face was conflicted with emotions as tears brimmed from his eyes. I knew he felt he had to leave and be there for his wife, but what about me? What about the baby that we were having? Okay, so we weren't really having a baby. But we would be once I figured out how I was going to get that baby away from his bitch ass wife, Tiffani. The wheels in my head began to turn as my mind strategized a plan to get her baby and make it mine. I just hoped she wasn't lying too.

There was no way she was going to take my man back. He was mine and we were going to be together, even if that meant getting rid of Tiffani's ass. As I led my man back in the house, I hoped that I could figure this shit out soon. I wished I hadn't said that I was pregnant, but now that I had, I would have to come through with a solid plan to take that baby away from his bitchy wife. She wasn't going to have him. Not as long as I could still breathe air in my lungs. These next few months should be real interesting.

Chapter ten

Lincoln

I just got back from work two days ago and already my life was in chaos and turmoil. Yesterday, I left Maddie's apartment and went to the house I shared with Tiffani. I was going to pick up the rest of my clothes and take them to Maddie's. I had already filed for a divorce two weeks ago, so the most logical step was for me to move out, right? At least, that was what I thought. I arrived at Tiff's place and she was sitting on the sofa with her feet curled under her. When I walked through the door, she didn't bother to get up and greet me, which was cool because I didn't need her to.

"Hey," I greeted her as I sat down in the chair across from her. I wanted to make sure not to sit next to her because I didn't want her to try and throw herself at me again. But, we also needed to have a conversation.

I needed her to know that it wasn't okay to drop by Maddie's place anytime she felt like it. That was a no no. I mean, Maddie didn't come over here to pick on her or cause her any problems, so she should give her the same respect. I knew she thought that Maddie had stolen me from her, but she needed to know that wasn't true. Maddie didn't steal me from her because I was never hers to begin with.

"Hey. I'm glad you came by," she said as she looked at me. She smiled at me and I could tell there was something different about her.

"I came by to get the rest of my things, but we need to talk," I said.

"I know."

"First of all, I need you to stop going by Maddie's apartment…"

"She broke up our marriage!"

"NO!" I said a little louder than I intended. "She didn't break our marriage up. I wanted to end things with you since the first day I saw her again. I hadn't seen her in years and when I finally laid eyes on her again, I was smitten; just the same way I was on that first day we met. It was like I was drawn to her again. It was all me, not her. I pursued her, not the other way around."

"She still didn't say no! You're still wearing your wedding ring, so she knew you were married and she still…"

"She said no."

"What?" she asked in a surprised tone.

"She did tell me no, but I wouldn't listen. I continued to chase her until I got her. I'm sorry because I never meant to hurt you. I planned to have a conversation with you about it before you found out from somebody else. But, as it turned out, you found out on your own. You need to stop blaming her because none of this is her fault. It's my fault. I'm the one that's married to you and I stepped out on you. I went against our vows," I said.

She was in tears by the time I finished the last sentence and I felt bad about making her cry, but she had to know. She stood up and walked over to the table in the corner. She picked up the yellow envelope, which I assumed held our divorce papers in them. She returned to the sofa and sat down. "So, you really want a divorce?" she asked me sadly.

"Yes. I've told you this a long time ago. I'm in love with someone else. Us staying together would only hurt you in the long run," I said.

"But, what if I don't want a divorce? I love you, Lincoln... from the bottom of my heart, I really do!" she cried.

"But, I don't want to be married to you anymore. Do you want me to stay married to you even though that's not what I want?"

"So, you're really going to divorce me and let me raise our child by myself?"

"I don't want to be..." The words that she had spoken hit me like a ton of bricks. "What did you say?"

"I asked if you're really going to divorce me and let me raise our child by myself."

I knew I had heard something about a child, but I was hoping that I had misunderstood. I looked at her and she was practically glowing. She pulled a yellow paper from the envelope and handed it to me. I read the paper and it stated that she had gone to the doctor's office last week and was indeed pregnant. She handed me a sonogram with her name on it. It stated that she was approximately ten weeks along and due in March.

My mouth literally hit the damn floor. How could she be pregnant? I didn't even remember the two of us having sex. The only pussy that had been on my mind and lips was Maddie's. Tiffani's pussy was so far from my mind, I didn't even remember what it looked like. She was pregnant. Damn. I really didn't see that shit coming at all.

"You're pregnant?" I asked with what I was sure was confusion on my face.

"Yes! We're pregnant! Aren't you happy?" she asked.

What kind of fucking question was that? She asked was I happy. "Tiff, are you kidding me right now?" I asked. "You're asking me if I'm happy about you being pregnant. I filed for divorce! How am I supposed to be happy when I filed for divorce from you? I mean, this marriage isn't even a marriage anymore!"

She stood up and came to kneel before me. "Lincoln, I feel that this is God's way of giving us a second chance at saving our marriage. He's given us another baby. This baby is a blessing for us and I know that we can be happy again. We can get back to how we used to be before you started screwing that girl. Please, Lincoln... please, give us another chance. I don't wanna raise this baby by myself. I want us to be a family," she said as she held onto my hand and stared in my face. I didn't want to be with this woman. I didn't even love her anymore. Over the past few months, I couldn't wait to get away from her. I wanted out of this marriage.

"We took vows before our friends, family, and the pastor that said for better or worse. We owe it to ourselves and our baby to try and make the worse better. I love you so much and I promise if you come back home, I won't ever mention your infidelity again. It'll be like it never happened," she said.

"I don't know what to say," I said.

"Please, Lincoln. We're having a baby."

"I'll be back."

I stood up from the chair and walked towards the front door. "Where are you going?" she cried from behind me.

"I need some space. I'll be back."

I hopped in my truck and backed out of the driveway. As soon as I was down the street, I called Josiah. I needed to talk to my best friend because I didn't know what to do. I was in love with Maddie and she was the one I wanted to be with. I didn't want to be with Tiffani anymore. I had her served with the divorce papers for a reason.

"Wassup, bro?" Josiah asked when he answered the phone.

"Yo, what you doing? I need to come over and talk to you, if you not too busy," I said.

"Nah, we ain't too busy. C'mon over."

"I'm on my way," I said.

Twenty minutes later, I pulled into their driveway. I chirped the alarm and walked up to the door. He opened the door and let me in without me having to knock or ring the bell. One look at my face and he knew something was wrong.

"What's wrong, bro? You look like you lost your best friend," he said.

"Lawd, lemme get a drink first," I said.

"Yea sure. What you want?"

"The strongest shit you got."

"Damn! It must be really bad!" he said.

"Hell yea, it is!"

I watched as he poured us each a glass of Patron. It wasn't a shot glass either. It was a glass that was more than halfway full, but I needed that shit. As I sat in the chaise, he sat down across from me on the sofa. I took a big gulp of my drink as Nova walked in.

"Hey, Lincoln!" she greeted me with a quick hug.

"Wassup, Nova?"

"Oh Lord, y'all are both drinking. What's wrong?" she asked.

"I'm trying to figure that out," Josiah said.

"Do you want me to leave? Was this supposed to be a private conversation?" Nova asked.

"No, you don't have to go. I could use all the ears I can get because I need advice," I said.

"What's going on?"

"Okay, so y'all know that I moved in with Maddie, right?" I asked.

Nova looked shocked, but didn't say anything negative. "Yea, so what happened? Did the two of you get in an argument?"

"No, no… Maddie and I are doing great! I love her more than I've ever loved any other woman before in my life."

"Then what's the problem?" Josiah asked.

"I went by my place earlier to get some more of my shit to take to Maddie's. When I got there, I sat down because me and Tiff needed to talk. She had gone by Maddie's place and I needed her to know that she was overstepping her boundaries when she did that," I said.

"Tiffani was overstepping her boundaries?" Nova asked almost in shock.

"Yea, cuz she can't just show up at Maddie's place like that, uninvited and shit!"

"I'm not trying to start no shit, I promise. But, wasn't Maddie overstepping when she started sleeping with you knowing that you and Tiff were married?" Nova asked.

She was the last person I expected to ask a question like that. I mean, Maddie was supposed to be her best friend. So, if Maddie was her best friend, why was she taking Tiffani's side? I was a grown ass man and anything that happened between me and Maddie was because I wanted it to happen.

"Whatever happened between me and Maddie, your best friend, was because I wanted it to."

"I know she's my best friend," Nova said, taking a defensive tone.

"Then act like it! Anyway, I was talking to her and she broke out with the DIVORCE papers I had her served with," I said as I looked at Nova.

"You actually filed for divorce?" she asked.

"Yes, I wouldn't have moved in with Maddie if I hadn't taken that step."

"So, what happened? Did she sign the papers?" Josiah asked.

"I thought that was why she was getting them, but she handed me a paper instead," I said as I ran my hands down my face.

"What is it, bro? Don't tell me she has a disease or something," Josiah said.

"She's pregnant!" I blurted before I lost my nerve.

Josiah started choking on his drink and shit. He was choking so bad that Nova started patting him on the back. When he was finally in control, I asked, "You aight?"

"Yea. That shit just went down the wrong way," he said as he wiped his teary eyes.

"So, Tiffani is pregnant?" Nova asked.

"Yea," I confirmed.

"Wow! How far along is she?" Josiah asked.

"About ten weeks."

"That's so crazy. I'm pregnant too," Nova said.

"What?! Wow! How far along?" I asked.

"We don't know yet," Josiah said. "She has an appointment in a couple of days for an ultrasound."

"That's great! Congratulations!" I said as I stood up to hug them. I was truly happy for them and wished that it was Maddie and I with the same news instead of me and Tiffani.

"So, what's going on with you and Tiffani? Are you going back to her to help her through the pregnancy?" Nova asked.

"Yea, bro. Whatchu gonna do?" Josiah asked.

"I don't know. That's what brought me here. I need some advice. I wanna be with Maddie, but Tiffani is having my baby. What the fuck should I do, yo?" I asked.

"You're going to look so heartless if you just divorce her while she's pregnant," Nova said.

"I know and that's the shit I don't like. I don't want people looking at me like I'm the bad guy. I don't even remember fucking her, that's the crazy part. Maybe she was fucking somebody else because I don't remember putting my dick in her at all," I said.

"All it takes is one time," Nova said.

Fuck! And that one time just popped in my fucking head too. Dammit! I wished I could turn back the hands of time because now I had to break Maddie's heart. Why was God punishing me this way? All I wanted was to be with the woman I loved…

Chapter eleven

Tiffani

When I found out that I was pregnant, I was stunned. I hadn't had sex with my husband in almost three months. I couldn't believe that the one time we had sex, I got pregnant. He hadn't been giving me any dick since he had been giving it to that homewrecking bitch, but one day, he caught me in a vulnerable state and one thing led to another. I was crushed when he left me as soon as we were done having sex, but what could I do about it?

I hadn't been feeling well, so I decided to go to the doctor. When he said that I was pregnant, you could have heard a pin drop in that room. That was the last thing I expected him to tell me, but it was also the best thing he could have told me. A baby was the answer to my prayers. A baby could save my marriage.

When Lincoln left after hearing the news about my pregnancy, I didn't know if he would be coming back. He said he would be back, but I wasn't sure. I was nervous when he left because I knew if he was going to Maddie's house, she would somehow talk him into staying with her. But, how could he abandon me when I was pregnant with our child? That was the one thing that I could give him that she hadn't yet. I got pregnant by him first. I knew that he would do the right thing.

I waited for him until ten o'clock and finally went to bed. I was ready to cry myself to sleep when I heard the door to the laundry room open. I almost shitted in my underwear with excitement when he walked in our bedroom. I couldn't help but smile at seeing him. He, on the other hand, didn't look as happy as I was.

"You're back!" I said, not being able to contain my happiness.

"I told you I would be back," he said. His response was so dry when he spoke to me.

"What does that mean?"

"What does what mean, Tiff?" he asked as he exhaled loudly.

"The fact that you're here right now?" I asked.

"It means that I'm here. You're pregnant and we're married, so I'm here," he said.

"Did you break up with her?"

"I'd rather not talk about my relationship with her right now."

"But, I need to know if you're here because you're going to give our marriage another chance. I'm hoping that you're here for myself as well as for our child."

"Look, I'm here, okay? Let's just leave it at that. I'm going to take a shower," he said as he rummaged through the drawers for some under clothes. I was confused by his presence. I was happy that he was here, but confused at the same time.

I wanted to believe that he was here to make our marriage work. When he finished taking his shower, he got in on his side of the bed and turned his back towards me. I guess he was here just for the sake of our baby. I wondered if I would be able to live in a marriage like that. I guess I would see how things worked out for us.

****

The next morning, I woke up to a text message from Nova.

Nova: Congratulations, girl! Lincoln told us that y'all were expecting!

Me: Thank you so much!

Nova: When are you due?

Me: March

Nova: Great! Maybe we'll be due around the same time

Wait a minute! Did she say that maybe we would be due at the same time?

Me: Are you pregnant too?

Nova: Yep

Me: Wow! I didn't know… congratulations to y'all as well!!

Nova: Thank you! We are so happy!

Me: So, Josiah is happy too?

Nova: Yaaassss! He can't wait for us to go to the doctor for an ultrasound.

Me: Lucky you… Lincoln couldn't care less about my pregnancy

Nova: Give him some time. He'll come around

Me: You really think so? He told me that he's in love with Maddie. How can I even compete with that?

Nova: Because you're his wife and carrying his child

Me: I hope that's enough

Nova: Give him some time... good luck

Me: Thanks

We stopped texting after that. I appreciated the encouragement with my husband. I would have thought that since she was Maddie's best friend, she would have been with her. But, for whatever reason she was offering me signs of hope with my man and marriage, I was grateful.

Lincoln emerged from the bathroom dressed and ready to go. I was curious as to where he was going, but was too afraid to ask. I knew if I asked and didn't like the answer, it would open the water works. I had been crying a whole lot lately, but my doctor said it was just my hormones. I just wanted my marriage back to the way it once was.

"I'll be back later," Lincoln said as he grabbed his keys.

I didn't respond to that. What was I going to say? He started his truck and backed out of the garage. I just sat there and once again, the tears started. I loved my husband, but I didn't know how much of this I could take.

Maybe as I got further along in my pregnancy and he started attending the appointments with me, he would understand how real it was. I prayed that things would get better between us.

"Lord, if you're listening to me, please grant me the strength to get through this pregnancy with or without my husband. As much as I love him and want to save our marriage, I'm gonna need you to guide me in the right direction. Please give me a sign that I'm doing the right thing. Please help me. In Jesus name, Amen."

As I thought about the pregnancy, a thought hit me. It was something I hadn't thought about since it happened, but thinking about it now could ruin everything. I had totally forgotten about sleeping with Josiah that day. The same day I slept with my husband.

"Oh my God! What if…"

I didn't dare say the words. I couldn't say them because if I spoke them out loud, it would make the possibility more real. I couldn't think of that right now. This baby was my husband's and no one else's. It had to be…

Chapter twelve

Josiah

How the fuck could this shit have happened? Sleeping with Tiffani was the worst mistake of my damn life. How could I have allowed myself to be that weak for some pussy that was off limits like a muthafucka? I should never have fucked that woman, but she knew what she was doing when she opened Pandora's box like that.

Now, not only was Nova pregnant by me, but there was a possibility that my best friend's wife might be carrying my child too. If Nova ever found this shit out, she would kill me and I would deserve it. She was a great woman and I should have never crossed that line with Tiffani. I was happy as any man would be to find out that the woman he loved was carrying his child. I loved Nova more and more every single day and I wanted to spend my life with her.

But, finding out that Tiffani was pregnant too. "God, help us all if that baby turns out to be mine," I prayed.

"You said something, baby?" Nova asked as she walked in the room.

"Oh, naw! Just humming a song that's stuck in my head," I lied.

"Oh, okay. Are you excited about being a daddy?" she asked as she came over to sit on my lap.

"Yea, I'm very excited!" I said as I kissed her.

"You are going to make a wonderful daddy."

She was beaming and glowing at the same time. She looked so beautiful. My guts twisted in turmoil because I hated lying to her. I wanted to tell her that I had slipped up and fucked Tiffani, but I couldn't risk losing her. Nova was my life and I knew if she ever found out, she would leave me. Not to mention, if Smoke found out. Smoke and I had been friends forever and I didn't want to lose his friendship. We were more like brothers instead of best friends. I would give him the shirt off my back, just as he would do for me.

"I texted Tiffani this morning to congratulate her. She's worried that Smoke isn't happy about their baby. I told her to just give him some time and that he'd come around," she smiled.

Nova was always so optimistic about everything. That was one of the main reasons why I loved her so much. "That was nice of you to offer her some hope, but I don't think that nigga is gonna come around that much. His heart ain't in his marriage no more. I don't see how he plans to stay with Tiff until she gives birth when he loves Maddie. That's gotta be a hard pill to swallow. His mom was pissed to find out that he had left Tiff to go stay with his "side chick" as she called Maddie. She lit into his ass! I think that was his main reason for going back home to Tiff," I said.

"As much as I love Maddie, Smoke is already married, and he belongs with his pregnant wife," Nova said. Her phone started ringing so she looked at it. I could see Maddie's face on the screen as she slid to accept the call.

"Hey girl," she answered.

I couldn't hear what Maddie was saying, but she sounded excited. "Wait... what?!"

"Oh my God! You're pregnant?! Are you sure?" she looked over at me and mouthed the words, "Maddie's pregnant too."

I slapped my forehead with my hand as I leaned back against the chair. How the hell was Smoke going to handle two women being pregnant? What was he going to do now that Maddie was pregnant too? I wondered what he was going to tell his family. Damn. That shit just got real for my nigga.

Nova ended the call with Maddie and looked at me. "Maddie is pregnant too?" I asked.

"Can you believe it? I mean, what are the odds that Smoke would have two women pregnant at the same damn time?" she asked.

"Damn! I know my boy must be shitting on himself! Two women pregnant!"

"Maddie said that he left her to go back to Tiffani, which we already knew."

"She sounded like she was excited," I said.

"No, she was actually crying. She said she really loves Smoke and will do anything to get him back. I can understand how she feels now that I know she's pregnant. No woman wants to raise a child alone. But, she put herself in that situation as soon as she laid down with Smoke knowing that he was married," Nova said. I was surprised that she was being so hard on Maddie concerning Smoke.

You couldn't help who you fell in love with. I knew I couldn't.

"You can't help who you love, baby. I'm sure they didn't plan to hurt Tiffani, but shit happens. You knew that the two of them had an attraction to each other since they first met. The same way I had an attraction to you even when I saw you checking Smoke out."

She hid her face behind her hands. "You saw that?" she asked, embarrassed.

"Yea, but I knew he was digging your best friend and I was digging you. Everything happened for a reason though and I truly believe that you and I were made for each other. I know for a fact that you're my soulmate. I can't wait to have this baby with you," I said.

"I'm so glad you're excited. I was nervous because we had never spoke about having babies. I wasn't sure how you were gonna feel about the baby when I told you. I feel like I got the better man when you chose me. That could have been me instead of Maddie," she said.

"That could never be you. You're the only woman for me and I'll always love you. Nobody ever got me the way that you do, baby."

I meant that shit too. I loved Nova more than I had ever loved any other woman I ever fucked with. She was special from the first day I met her. I knew that I was going to be with her. I planned on asking her to marry me for Christmas, but now that she was pregnant, I think I wanna ask her sooner than that. I was thinking maybe before I left to go back to work.

"I gotta go get dressed for work," she said as she slid off my lap.

"Already?"

"Yea, I had to switch shifts with Elena so I could take off tomorrow for my ultrasound. Her shift is always two hours earlier than mine," she said.

Well, that was just the excuse I needed to make my way to the jewelry store. I followed her into the bedroom. "What are you going to do while I'm gone?"

"I don't know. I'm kinda tired from all that good good you put on me last night. I might take a nap then go chill with the fellas."

"Okay, just know that I'll be thinking about you while I'm at work," she said with a smile. I walked over to her and tilted her head up with my finger on her chin.

"That's good because I'm always thinking about you." I brought my lips down to hers and inserted my tongue in her mouth.

"Mmmm! Boy, you need to stop before I'm late."

"Aight. I'ma let you get ready. I love you, babe," I said as I kissed her on the temple.

"I love you too."

She went ahead and got dressed and I put some plans in motion to go get the ring. Right after I had kissed my baby goodbye, I got a text message. I pulled my phone out and swiped to unlock my phone. The text was from Tiffani and I wondered why she was texting me.

Tiffani: Hey, I know that Nova is pregnant, and I also know that Lincoln told you I am too. Please keep what happened between us a secret. I want to save my marriage, so I told him that the baby is his. I don't really know if it's yours or his, but I want my marriage to work

Me: Y the hell r u texting me w/ this bs?

Tiffani: I just wanted to make sure we were on the same page

Me: WTF r u talkin' bout?

Tiffani: U know

Me: Look, maybe it's best if we don't communicate like this anymore. If we meet up as a group, fine. But, don't text or call me no more

Tiffani: Sorry. I was just…

I didn't finish reading it. I blocked her number because she didn't seem to get it. Even though I knew exactly what she was referring too, I was going to play the retarded bastard from here on out. I didn't want to hear shit about that day we fucked. I didn't want to hear shit about her pregnancy or her keeping what happened a secret. As far as I was concerned, if the shit got out, it would be her word against mine and seeing as how me and Smoke been brothers since forever, there wasn't a doubt in my mind that he would believe me over her.

If she had anything to say concerning the baby she was carrying, she needed to be talking to her husband, not texting me. I was out of that equation. My concern was with my woman and our child that she was carrying. I left the house and made sure the door was locked. The last thing I needed was for Tiffani to be hiding and waiting for me when I returned. I knew just where I wanted to get my baby's ring too. So, I headed straight to Zales.

As I was pulling into the parking lot, my phone started to ring. Smoke's number popped up on my screen, so I clicked the button to take the call.

"Wassup, bro? You got everything squared away?" I asked. I didn't want to mention shit about Maddie's pregnancy. I decided to wait until he said something first.

"Nah bro. I found out yesterday that Maddie is pregnant too!" he said. I could tell from the tone of his voice that he was definitely stressed. Hell, I would be stressed too if I were in his shoes.

"Damn! You got yo wife and side chick pregnant?!"

"Maddie isn't my side chick, yo! I love her. I am in love with her! What the fuck did I do wrong? I know what the fuck I did, I should have never married Tiffani. That's where I fucked up," he said.

"Damn! I'm sorry if I offended you about that side chick comment. I didn't mean nothing by it. Whatchu gonna do?" I asked.

"I don't know what to do. I had gone back to Tiff because you and my mom said it was the right thing to do. But, how can I support Tiff with her pregnancy and not do the same for Maddie? She's the one I love and wanna be with. This whole situation is fucked up!" he said.

"Yea, it really is, especially if it's keeping you from being with the one you really love. I shouldn't have told you to go back to Tiffani if she isn't who you wanna be with. Where is it written that you can't support her and be with Maddie? I mean, you already filed for the divorce, right?"

"Yea, but I tried explaining that shit to my mom and she almost beat me like when I was a kid. She ain't having that shit. She said since I'm married to Tiffani, I need to stay with her."

"Have you told her that Maddie's pregnant too?"

"Hell no! My mom would beat the black off my ass if she knew that shit!" he said.

"Well bro, I think you should let her know. Your mom knows everybody in this damn town. If you don't tell her, eventually, she's gonna find out from somebody else and you don't want them troubles," I said.

"Yea, I know."

"How far along is Maddie?"

"About ten or eleven weeks, same as Tiffani. Damn!" he said. I could tell that he was angry.

"Where are you now?"

"Driving around, trying to stay away from Maddie. Whatchu got going on?" he asked.

"I was about to walk in Zales and get a ring for my baby," I said with a smile.

"Whaaattt?! You about to ask Nova to marry you?"

"Yea, she's having my baby and I love her."

"That's great, bro. Just make sure if you're going to marry her, that she's the one you're IN LOVE with. Don't make the same mistake I made," he advised.

"Oh, trust me, I'm not. Nova is my soulmate and there's no other woman in this world for me except her," I said.

"Aight. Well, I'ma hit you up later then. Go handle yo business."

"Yea, aight. Maybe we can go shoot some hoops later," I said.

"Yea, maybe."

We ended the call and I kinda felt sorry for my best friend. I wished he and Maddie had gotten together from the jump, so all of this extra bullshit could have been avoided. Now, he had himself in a pickle with not only his wife pregnant, but Maddie too. I sure hoped that he was able to find a solution to that problem soon. However, I didn't see any easy way out.

"Good afternoon, welcome the Zales! Is there anything in particular that you're looking for?" the salesperson asked when I walked through the door.

As I looked at the beautiful ring sets, all thoughts of Smoke and his problems vanished from my mind. The only thing on my mind now was proposing to Nova before I left to go back to work. I loved her and my life...

Chapter thirteen

Maddie

I wished I hadn't blurted out to Lincoln that I was pregnant. Now, I had to go through the motions of pretending that I was pregnant. I got online and found a website that sold fake pregnancy bellies. They came in silicone and foam, so I ordered the silicone one. I wasn't a big girl, so I could pass this pregnancy off for five months before I started showing. I hated lying to Lincoln, but there was no way I was giving up on us. He told me that he loved me and I loved him. Why couldn't Tiffani just disappear? That would make everything so simple for us.

But, I knew all too well that God had to make sure you had the strength to take the good with the bad. I definitely had what it took, but he may not like how I handled things. The devil on the other hand, had been high fiving me since he figured out what I was going to do. It was like I had a good angel on one shoulder and that little red devil on the other. But, that lil devil was talking to me a lot more than the angel.

I was totally heartbroken that Lincoln chose to go back to that bitch, Tiffani. I mean, he had filed for a divorce. I just didn't get why his mom wanted him to support a wife he was divorcing. I can bet it was because she didn't know about me, but she would. I didn't want to rat Lincoln out that way, but we were in love, so we should be together.

Once I thought about it, I wondered how I would hide the fact that I wasn't really pregnant away from him if I fought to keep him with me. I loved Lincoln, but if this was going to work, we couldn't be together until after the "baby" was born.

KNOCK! KNOCK! KNOCK!

I didn't know who that was, so I braced myself because if it was Tiffani at my door again, so help me God. I was going to fuck her up. I opened the door to find Lincoln standing there, looking as good as he wanted to be. I smiled at him as our eyes locked.

"I'm sorry, but I couldn't stay away," he said.

I simply backed out of the doorway, so he could enter. Our eyes remained locked on each other's as he closed the door and stepped closer to me. In one swift motion he had picked me up like a little kid. I wrapped my legs around him as we kissed each other hungrily. We didn't even make it to the living room. He placed me on the kitchen counter and removed my panties, diving in to eat my goodies.

I ran my fingers through his hair as he went to munching. "Oh shit!" I cried out as I held on to the cabinet door. I was glad I had on my night clothes, panties, and one of Lincoln's shirts that he left behind. After I gushed into his mouth, he quickly dropped his pants and boxers and entered me. That was the first time that we had sex on the countertop in the kitchen, but it wouldn't be the last.

I rode the dick like it was the last one on earth. I creamed all over his dick as we continued to hold on to each other. "I love you so much," I crooned in his ear.

"I love you too," he said.

He lifted me off the counter and fucked me standing up. This had become one of his and my favorite positions. I loved how he clutched my ass cheeks and drove his dick into my wet pussy at the same time. He made me feel so amazing. Whatever I was doing was in the name of love, even if it meant committing the ultimate sin.

I held on to him as he fucked me like it was our first time. When he pulled me closer and he began grinding into me, I thought I was going to lose my mind. That was the first time he had ever done me that way. "Oh my God! That feels soooo good!" I moaned.

"Mmmmm hmmm!" he moaned.

He walked me over to the living room and placed my butt on the arm of the sofa. He climbed on top of me and dipped low. His dick felt so good. No wonder Tiffani wanted to fight me for it, but she could fight until her last breath and she wouldn't win. Lincoln was standing up with a grip on my hips as he plowed inside me. All I could do was scream in pleasure. He took me to ecstasy before, but never like this.

After I don't know how long, he succumbed to his feelings of pleasure and sprayed my insides, yet again. Oh my God! He leaned into me and kissed me, but a sudden feeling of nausea took over and I quickly pushed him off of me. I rushed to the bathroom and made it just in time to throw myself over the toilet and puke my guts out. Lincoln had followed me and was holding my hair back.

"I guess that's part of being pregnant, huh?" he said.

"Yep," I said when I was done. I wasn't pregnant, so it had to be some sort of stomach virus. "Ugh! I hate throwing up!"

"It's okay, baby. You're throwing up for a good damn reason," he said as he flushed the toilet while I rinsed my mouth with water. I grabbed the mouthwash and poured some in the top before swishing it in my mouth for about three minutes.

I walked out of the bathroom to find Lincoln arguing on the phone with Tiffani. "I'll come home when I'm ready. Don't worry about where I am!"

When he saw me, he ended the call and placed the phone in his pocket. "Let me guess who that was," I said.

"Let you not. I don't want to think about her while I'm with you," he said. "When is your next doctor's appointment? Did you get a sonogram done to find out how far along you are?"

Those were questions I wasn't expecting him to ask after we just had mind blowing sex. I sat next to him on the sofa and tried to make my brain function to give him some answers. "My next doctor's appointment is in two weeks." I picked that time because I knew he would be back on water for work, so he wouldn't be able to come. "As for a sonogram, I won't have one of those for a few more weeks. They were able to give me an expected due date from my last period."

"When are you due?"

"Um, they said sometime around the middle of March. They won't know for sure until I have an ultrasound..."

"I would love to go with you to that appointment, so could you please schedule it when I'm home?" he asked.

"Yea, sure." I mouthed the words and heard them come out, but on the inside, I was wondering how I was going to pull this shit off. "I'll ask my doctor next time I see her."

KNOCK! KNOCK! KNOCK!

We looked at each other before we went to the door to see who was knocking so hard. I pulled the door open as he stood over my shoulder. Tiffani was once again standing on my doorstep. "I knew you were over here!" she fussed as she looked at Lincoln.

"Why are you here?" I asked.

"I came for my husband!" she said as she looked over my shoulder at Lincoln. He rolled his eyes and sucked his teeth. "Lincoln, let's go!"

"Tiffani, I'm not your fuckin' kid and you can't tell me what to fuckin' do! I told you not to come back over here!" he said.

"WHY SHOULDN'T I COME HERE?! YOU DON'T WANT THIS HOMEWRECKIN' BITCH'S NEIGHBORS TO KNOW THAT MY HUSBAND IS HERE AGAIN!! WELL, THAT'S TOO DAMN BAD!" she yelled.

"You need to stop hollering in the front of my apartment before I call the police on your ass. I was trying not to get you locked up because of your condition, but keep fuckin' with me and I won't have a choice!" I said through clenched teeth.

"All I want is my husband and I'm outta here. And tell me this... if you know of my "condition" as you called it, why are you still fucking him?" she sneered as she rubbed her belly.

"That's easy," I said as I rubbed my belly. "I have the same condition, so you might as well get used to him being over here."

Her mouth dropped open and tears clouded her eyes. I was glad I had gotten a reaction like that outta her ass. That shit was hilarious and I would have cracked up had it not been for my neighbors. The last thing I wanted was to get put out of this apartment for excessive noise and I knew this bitch wouldn't hesitate to make a scene.

"Lincoln, you got her pregnant?" she asked, hurt written all over her face.

"That wasn't my intention, but yes, she is pregnant."

"So, what are you going to do? I'm pregnant and your side bitch is pregnant! I can't believe you're doing this to our marriage!" she cried.

"Lincoln, I need her off of my doorstep, baby. Like, right now," I said as I turned to him.

He went to the kitchen and picked up his t-shirt. He put it on and kissed me, "I'll be back." I couldn't believe he did that right in her face. From the look on her face, neither could she. He stepped out and grabbed her by the arm, pulling her towards her car. I didn't know what was going on with them, but I knew that Lincoln would handle her ass. She was so desperate and it was starting to show.

These next few months were going to be a little more difficult than I thought.

Another wave of nausea sent me running to the bathroom, but thankfully, I didn't throw up that time. I was going to have to get that shit checked.

****

Two days later, I sat in the exam room of my doctor's office, ready to find out why I had been feeling so under the weather. Lincoln had taken his mom to the doctor for a check-up so I was grateful for that. The last thing I needed was him following me over here for them to tell him that I wasn't pregnant. I had pissed in a cup, had blood drawn and all my vitals taken.

A few minutes later, the doctor and nurse walked in the room. "Hi Maddie, how are you feeling today?" Doctor Norris asked.

"I haven't been feeling myself, Doctor Norris. I think I'm coming down with some kind of stomach virus or something," I said.

"Well, it has something to do with your stomach, but it's not a virus."

I looked at her with a confused look on my face. "What do you mean?"

"I mean, you're having a baby!" she blurted.

I almost fell off that damn exam table. I mean, sure, I wanted to keep Lincoln with a baby, but I wanted to take that bitch's baby. I didn't know that I was pregnant too. This shit was unbelievable.

"Come again."

"You're pregnant!" she said again. "I can see that you're surprised to hear that, but if you've been engaging in unprotected sex, I don't see how this surprises you."

"I-I-I just didn't expect it," I said in total shock. "Are you sure?"

"As sure as I can be. The urinalysis and blood test both confirmed it. You are definitely with child," she said. "Now, from the time of your last period, I'm thinking you're about fifteen weeks along. That would put your due date around sometime in February."

I was having a baby and my baby was due before Tiffani's. Oh my God! I was still winning! "Is there any way that I can get an ultrasound done within the next few days?"

"Well, usually we don't schedule ultrasounds until your fourth month. But, I can arrange that seeing as how you're about fifteen weeks now. That way, we can give you a more accurate due date and check to make sure your baby is doing okay. I will have my receptionist schedule it for you and she will give you a call by this afternoon or early morning," Doctor Norris said.

"Thanks so much, Doctor Norris. I really appreciate this!" I said.

"No problem. I'll also recommend an OB for you as well," she said.

"Okay, thanks. On second thought, that's okay, my best friend is pregnant, so I'll go with her to see her OB. That way, we can share this experience together."

"Great! If you could take this chart to my receptionist, she'll check you out and schedule your appointment for the ultrasound."

I left her office feeling happier than I had ever felt before in my life. I couldn't believe how this shit had played out. I couldn't wait to share this news with Lincoln. I called him as soon as I got in my car.

"Hey babe," he answered.

"Hey, are you busy?" I asked.

"Never too busy for you. Wassup?"

"I was able to get an ultrasound scheduled for tomorrow. The doctor is going to call me back with the time, so I hope you can make it," I said.

"Hell yea, I can make it! I'm so excited!" he said.

"I knew you would be. That's why I was happy that she was able to make the appointment before you left for work. Am I gonna be able to see you later?" I asked.

"Yep. I'll come by in about an hour or so," he said.

"Great! I love you, Lincoln."

"I love you, too."

We ended the call and I smiled at how God worked his magic. I guess all I had to do was have faith and he would handle everything else. I flicked my finger over my left shoulder to knock that lil devil off his perch. I didn't need his lil ass anymore, so he could now kick rocks.

Chapter fourteen

Tiffani

I knew that I would find my husband back at that bitch's house. What I wasn't expecting was to find him and her in the state that they were in. I could tell by their lack of clothing that they had just finished having sex. The sight of the two of them disgusted me. I wanted to jump on that bitch and beat her ass for fooling around with my husband. I wondered if he had told her that I was pregnant. If he had, she sure didn't give a fuck about that. I mean, if a bitch knew that the nigga that she was fooling around with had a wife, she should look for someone else. If she found out that his wife was pregnant, then why keep fucking with him?

That was so dumb and desperate to me. Out of all the single men in this world, she had to sink her talons into mine. I just couldn't understand why she didn't just admit she made a mistake and back away from him. I knew his dick was good, but damn.

Hearing her tell me that she was pregnant felt like a punch in the stomach. As if I wasn't reeling enough from that information, he had the nerve to kiss her while I was standing right there watching them. It made me feel like if she was the one he was married to and I was just some random bitch who wanted his attention. Why would my own husband continue to make me feel like shit, especially when I was pregnant?

As he pulled me to my car, I broke free of his grasp. "I can't believe you just did that!"

"Did what?" he asked as he shrugged his shoulders.

"You really just kissed that bitch in front of me! Why would you do that? Were you trying to make me feel like shit? Were you trying to hurt my feelings?" I asked.

"We'll talk about this at home. I'll follow you there," he said.

I got in my car and he in his truck and we made our way home. I was so hurt that I was getting blinded by my tears. I quickly swiped them away and paid attention to the road. Half an hour later, we pulled into the driveway of our home. I parked in the garage, but he didn't. Once we were inside, I was ready to continue our conversation.

"I asked you a question."

"And you expect me to remember that after I drove 30 minutes in traffic to get here?"

"I asked you if you kissed that bitch…"

"I'm gonna have to ask you to stop calling the mother of my child a bitch," he said as he raised his finger in my face.

"Do you defend me like that when she calls me out my name?" I asked.

"She never calls you a bitch, so I don't have to," he said. I knew he was lying, but for the sake of this conversation, I would do as he asked.

"Fine! Did you kiss her in my face to hurt my feelings?"

"I don't play those kinds of games. I kissed her because I wanted to and you just happened to be there. So, if anyone is responsible for your feelings getting hurt, it's you. Nobody told you to bring yo ass down here! As a matter of fact, I told you to stay away from her apartment! Didn't I?"

"Are you really making this my fault that I found you here?"

"No, I'm making it your fault that you got your feelings hurt! Look, I listened to my mom and Josiah…"

"Josiah? What the hell does he have to do with anything?"

"He's my best friend, so I asked for his advice…"

"You're asking him for advice?"

"Yea."

"About me?" I asked.

"What's wrong with that? I needed his opinion about how I should handle this pregnancy situation with you," he said.

"Oh, and let me guess, he told you to leave me, right?" I sneered. Typical nigga. I just knew Josiah was the reason that Lincoln was still messing with Maddie. I should have known from the jump and I should have gone after him for trying to turn my husband against me. If our little secret was to get out, it would fuck up his relationship with Nova. Hell, it would fuck up mine with my husband too, but the shit was already fucked up with Lincoln. I didn't have a damn thing to lose.

"As a matter of fact, he and my mom told me to honor my vows and stay with my wife."

"They said that?"

"Why do you sound so surprised? You know my mom likes you and knowing that you're pregnant made her team Tiff even more," he said.

"But, you're still here with her," I said as I pouted.

"Because I love her! Don't you get that? I wanted to do the right thing and stand by you, Tiff... I swear I did. But, knowing that Maddie is pregnant too made that impossible. I'm going through with the divorce. I'll pay my child support and help you raise our child, but I'm not moving back. I'm moving out," he said.

I saw his lips moving and I heard the words coming out, but the shattering sound of my heart breaking was louder than his words. I couldn't even respond to him once he said that. "Did you hear what I said, Tiff? I'm divorcing you and I'm moving out of the house," he repeated.

Tears flooded my eyes and it became hard for me to breathe. I was losing my husband. After everything I did to save our marriage, he was still leaving me. What could I do? "I love you, Lincoln. What am I supposed to do without you?"

"I'll still be there for you, Tiff. I'll still go with you to your doctor's appointments and ultrasounds. You'll just have to schedule them on my off weeks. I'll still help you pay for the mortgage until we sell the house," he said.

"Sell the house? You want to sell the house?" I asked. I loved my home. It was beautiful, and it had been my home for the last two years. I wasn't moving from my home. I wasn't selling my damn house.

"Well yea! We're getting a divorce and I won't be responsible for two mortgages."

"Two mortgages? That bitch pays rent!" I said, angry that he wanted us to sell our home.

"I asked you not to call her that and yes, Maddie pays rent now, but we'll eventually buy a house together. So, this house needs to go on the market."

"I'm not selling my house!"

"You don't have to. Since the house is in my name, I'll sell it!" he said.

"It's a marital asset. You can't sell it without my signature!" I said as I crossed my arms over my chest.

"I can sell it if it's in my name. I bought it without your signature and I can sell it without your signature. I'm selling the house and that's that!" he said.

He was right. He did buy the house without me and he told me it was for this very reason. He had told me that if our marriage didn't work, he didn't want to be stuck paying for this house after the divorce. I was so infatuated with him at the time I didn't realize he was planning to leave me. He played me this whole time.

"You've planned this all along, haven't you?" I asked.

"Planned what?"

"To leave me."

"No, but I've watched too many court shows to know better than to enter into a joint agreement as big as a home purchase. If shit doesn't work out, the husband is always the one to suffer the most. Having to pay for two places wasn't on my agenda."

"So, you're really doing this? You're really going to leave me and our baby and sell the house?" I asked.

"Yes."

He walked past me and made his way to the bedroom. I watched as he grabbed a suitcase and start putting all his clothes in them. "You're leaving now?" I asked as tears continued to stream down my face. I couldn't believe that he was just going to up and leave me. I wrapped my arms around his waist and buried my face in his back. "I love you, Lincoln. I love you so much. I'll do anything to save our marriage. Let's go to counseling, please. Just don't leave me!"

I could feel his stature tense up as he stood up straight. "Tiff, I can't live this life anymore with you. I'd be cheating myself out of a loving relationship just to please you. I can't do that."

"What am I supposed to do?"

"You'll get over this. Somewhere out there is a man just for you, but I'm not that man."

"I can't let you go!"

He removed my hands from around his waist and turned to look at me. "I would comfort you, but I remember all too well what happened the last time I did that, and I don't want a repeat session. I'm in enough trouble from the last time. But, you'll be fine," he said as he patted my shoulder.

"Fine, then go! GET THE HELL OUT!" I cried as I ran to the bathroom and locked the door. However, I could have left the door unlocked and I knew he wouldn't have come to see about me.

By the time I came out of the bathroom, he was gone. I slumped to the floor and curled myself up in a ball, crying my eyes out. My heart was literally broken and I was devastated.

****

A couple of hours later, I brushed myself off and decided to stop feeling sorry for myself. I needed to talk to the one person who I knew could help me get to Lincoln. I cleaned myself up, making myself more presentable. I left the house with only one thing on my mind, gaining an alliance to help me get my husband back.

I got in my car and made the thirty-minute drive to Josiah and Nova's house. I knew he was going to have a cow when he saw me, but I needed him to help me out. He needed to help me strategize to get my husband back because I wasn't giving up that easily. I loved my husband and we were having a child together. He needed to be at home with me, not running behind some lil hoochie mama.

I pulled into Josiah's driveway and his truck was there. I breathed a sigh of relief when I saw his truck in the driveway. I was hoping all the way here that I hadn't made this trip for nothing. I got out the car and made my way to the front door. I prayed that he wouldn't bring up our last encounter and hear me out. All I wanted was someone to help me save my marriage.

KNOCK! KNOCK! KNOCK!

I waited for him to come to the door and when he did, the smile he was wearing when I first saw him, disappeared. I could see that he was on the phone as he opened the door.

"Aye Smoke, I don't know what she's doing here when she knows my woman is at work, but I'ma need you to stop whatchu doing and come get your wife off my doorstep," he said into the phone.

I couldn't believe he was doing me that way. Not only was he shunning me, but he was doing it on the phone with my husband. I squinted my eyes at him as I gave him my mad dog face. "What the hell are you doing?" I mouthed softly.

"I'm letting your husband know that he needs to come get you. I already told you that my loyalty lies with Smoke." He stopped talking as he listened intently to my husband on the end of the line. "Yes, she's right here. You wanna talk to her? Hold on." He looked at me and said, "Your husband wants to speak to you." He handed me the phone and I yanked it from his palm. I couldn't believe that he had just did that. He didn't even give me a chance to tell him why I was here.

"Hello," I spoke into the phone.

"Tiffani, what the hell are you doing over there?!" Lincoln yelled into the phone.

"I came by to see if you were here," I lied.

"Oh really? I was just at the house a couple of hours ago. If you had something to say, you should have said it while I was there. You know how that shit looks… you going over to my boy's crib when his ol' lady ain't even there?" he fumed.

"What's it to you how it looks? It's not as if you care," I huffed.

"I do care because you could ruin his relationship doing bullshit like that!"

"You're worried about his relationship?! What about our relationship, Lincoln? When am I going to get some consideration? It just seems like you're worried about everybody else but me. When the hell are you going to give a damn about me?" I asked.

"Just take your ass home and get from round there. Damn! Why you always gotta make shit so damn difficult?"

"Oh, I'm sorry. I'm just a little distraught because my husband LEFT ME FOR HIS SIDE BITCH! AND YES, I MEANT TO SAY BITCH!" I yelled. I didn't even wait for him to say anything else. I ended the call and threw the phone at Josiah. "You fuckin' traitor!"

"Aye, if you break my damn phone, you best believe you gon' replace it. What the fuck you doing here?" he asked, but before I could answer, he stopped me. "Never mind! I don't care why you're here. Just leave and don't come back!"

"I bet you wouldn't be talking all that shit if Lincoln and your precious Nova knew that this baby could possibly be yours."

"You're crazy!" he spoke through clenched teeth. "Tell them! Tell them whatever you fuckin' want! You'll have to prove that's my baby and if it ain't, they gonna look at you like something's wrong witcho ass! So, go ahead and do it, but stay the fuck away from me!"

Having said that, he slammed his door shut in my face. I couldn't believe he and Lincoln were acting this way. I had one more person I could turn to and as I made my way over to her place, I couldn't help but smile. I knew if no one else in this damn city would help me, she would. It took me almost fifty minutes to get to Lincoln's mom's house. I didn't mind the drive though. I would have driven two hours if it meant she would be on my side.

I knocked on her door and she appeared in the doorway a couple of minutes later. A huge smile spread across her face when she saw me. "Hello Tiffani, come on in," she said as she unlocked the screen door.

"Hey momma, how are you?" I greeted her with a kiss on her cheek.

"I'm doing great. I was gonna call you because I'm a little worried about you. I spoke to Lincoln earlier," she said with a sympathetic look on her face.

"What did he tell you?"

"He told me that the two of you are getting a divorce."

"Did you tell him that you still think we should stay together, at least for the sake of our unborn baby?" I asked.

"I did tell him that, but you know what he told me? He said that he met someone and fell in love with her a long time ago. He said that he had been seeing her and that she's pregnant too. I was really shocked to hear that he had been sneaking around behind your back, but he asked that I let him live his life. As much as I love you, honey, I can't be involved in this situation. I have to let my son make his own decisions. But, just know that he did say he would always be there for you and he would see you through your pregnancy. I'll be here for you too because that is my grand baby that you're carrying," Ms. Rose said.

I loved Mama Rose like she was my own mother, and that was why I couldn't believe she was refusing to help me. "Mama Rose, please. I love my husband and I want us to raise our son or daughter as a family. You have to help me," I begged with tears in my eyes.

"Tiffani, you know I love you and I think that you're good for my son."

"Then please help me."

"I can't interfere in his relationship like that. He asked me to stay out of it and I have to respect that. I never thought my son would have two girls pregnant by him at the same time, but I promise to treat both of my grand babies the same. I'll do for them both and love them more. I wish I could help you, but my relationship with my son means the world to me," she said.

I hated that she wouldn't help me, but what else could I do? I had no choice but to go home and sign the divorce papers. I hoped and prayed that Lincoln would keep his word and be there for me during my pregnancy and after our child was born. I hugged his mom and left the house, broken and defeated. I love my husband and wished that he loved me as much as he loved that homewrecking bitch.

Chapter fifteen

Lincoln

Imagine my damn surprise when my boy, Josiah called me to tell me that Tiff was at his house. What the fuck was she even doing there?! Like, I done told her what I needed to tell her and she's still running around trying to get people on her side. I told her that I would be there for her through her pregnancy and I would step up and support my kid. I didn't know what else she wanted from me. But that was all I had for her. I couldn't stay with her when I was in love with someone else.

Had I not seen Maddie and we hadn't started this little fling, I would have had no problem staying with Tiffani. She was a good woman and I cared about her a whole lot. But, I had been craving Maddie since I blew that smoke in her face and she slapped the shit outta me. I tried to forget about her when she went away to college, and for a while, I had done a good job. I was even able to find happiness with Tiff, at least until I saw Maddie again.

That first night I laid eyes on her at the bar changed my life forever. It brought back all those feelings that I thought I had buried long ago. I thought I was over her, but as it turned out, I wasn't over Maddie; not by a long shot. When I first approached her and she found out that I was married, she told me she didn't want to be with me.

I had gone over to my mom's house because I needed her to know I had made a decision concerning my marriage. I just wanted to speak with her face to face so there wouldn't be any confusion. I knew that Tiffani was going to try and turn her against Maddie and I wasn't going to let that happen. I just needed her to know that I was really in love with Maddie. She was the one for me and Tiffani wasn't. No matter how much I wanted to do as my mom asked, I couldn't keep denying myself happiness for someone else.

I did a quick knock on her door before I let myself in. She was in the kitchen baking sweet potato pies for the church. That was my mom; always cooking or baking something. "Mmmmmm! It smells so good in here, ma!" I said as I kissed her cheek.

"Hey baby, what are you doing here?" she asked.

"I gotta have an excuse to come visit my mom?"

"No, baby. You never need an excuse to come see me. But, I know my child, and I know you got a reason for bringing yo'self all the way out here," she said.

"Maybe I came to take home one of these pies," I said. "It smells good, so I know you got one for your baby boy, huh?"

"Boy, you know this fa da church! God gon' know if I come up short on one of his pies," she said.

I sat at the table as she continued to work on her pies. "On the real, ma, I came by to talk to you about something. I need you to come sit with me when you get a chance."

She took her last pie out the oven and put in two more before coming to sit at the table with me. "What you need, baby? Something tells me this has to do with you and Tiffani," she said.

My mom knew me too well. She sat down next to me and patted me on the hand. "Come on, talk to mama."

"I met someone, ma."

"She sounds special," she said.

"She is… she really is. I've actually been knowing her for a while, but when we first met, I was a total ass to her."

"Well, what'd you do? Because I know I raised you better than that. I raised you to respect women, so please tell me what you did," she said in a stern voice.

I almost didn't want to tell her what I did to Maddie. I knew she would be upset with me, but I was sure she wouldn't mind the way things turned out between me and Maddie.

I shook my head from side to side as I got ready to talk to her. "Well, she asked me why they called me Smoke, so I blew smoke from my cigarette smoke in her face."

"Lincoooolln! Now you know better than that, boy!" she said as she popped me in the head.

"Ow ma! But wait, get this… she slapped the heck outta me!"

"Good for her!" my mom said.

"Ma! You're supposed to be on my side!" I said.

"I am always on your side, but you know better than to blow smoke in a woman's face; in anybody's face."

"I know, ma. I thought it woulda been something we could have laughed out. She didn't see it that way. She slapped me talkin' bout, 'Don't you ever disrespect me again!' She was so mad!" We had a good laugh at Maddie's reaction because I did it in such a dramatic fashion.

"Well, apparently she forgave you."

"She did, ma. We ran into each other about a year and a half ago. All those old feelings I had for her resurfaced. I tried my best to respect my vows and stay away from her, but I couldn't. I was just so drawn to her. From day one, we had a connection and absence made my heart grow fonder. She's the one, ma. I'm in love, like in love, for the first time in my entire life. I know how you feel about Tiff and my marriage to her, but I need you to be my mom and not her mother in law. I just want you to be happy for me." I said.

"So, what does that mean exactly?"

"It means that I'm divorcing Tiff and I wanna be with Maddie."

"But, your wife is pregnant! How can you leave her at a time like this to start over with someone else?" she asked.

"Well, that's the thing… and please, don't hit me." She gave me this funny look that said I would get it if she felt I needed it. "Maddie is pregnant too." I picked my hands up as soon as the words were out of my mouth. I needed to block the hit she was sure to rain down on me.

"I'm not gonna hit you, son. But, I need you to answer me one question."

"What's that?"

"How could you be so irresponsible to knock up two women at the same time? I know darn well yo daddy taught you how to wrap it up," she said.

"I just got caught up in the heat of the moment, ma. I know that you had that happen to you before, otherwise I wouldn't be here," I said as I cracked up with laughter.

"The difference between your dad and yourself is that I was the only one getting knocked up by him. You got two women having babies by you in the same year," she said.

"Yea, I know. I didn't mean for that to happen, it just did. But, I'm gonna be responsible and take care of both my kids. I told Tiff that I would be there for her throughout the pregnancy. I told her that I would go with her to her doctor's appointments and ultrasounds. I'm gonna be there for her, ma. I'm not gonna leave her to go through it by herself. You ain't raise me like dat," I said.

"I know I didn't. It seems as if you have everything thought out."

"So, do I have your blessing to divorce Tiff and be with Maddie?" I asked.

"As long as you're happy, baby, I'm happy."

We stood up and I pulled her in a tight embrace. "Thanks, ma."

"You ain't gotta thank me, baby. Every parent wants their child to be happy."

At the end of our talk, she gave me her blessing and a pie to take home. I loved my mom so much and couldn't wait to introduce her to Maddie. Soon as I got back to Maddie's place, I unloaded all my stuff that I was able to put into my truck in her apartment. As I looked around, the first thing that came to mind was that we needed a bigger place. As nice and luxurious and her apartment was, we were having a baby, so we needed to be comfortable. She wasn't home when I arrived, so I called to see where she was.

"Hey babe, are you at the apartment?" she asked.

"Yea, where you at?" I asked.

"I'm almost there. I stopped by the store and did a little shopping."

"Oh yea! What'd you buy at the store?"

"I'll show you when I get there," she said.

"Okay, hurry up! I got some good news for you," I said.

"I'm almost there."

"Aight babe," I said as we ended the call.

I couldn't wait for my baby to get home, so I could tell her that my mom gave us her blessing. As long as my mom did that, all was right with the world...

Chapter sixteen

Maddie

Four months later...

I was in my eighth month of pregnancy and as big as a damn blimp. I couldn't wait to give birth to our son next month. Lincoln and I had moved into a house two months ago. He was ready for us to move out of my small apartment, and so was I. We found a nice and spacious three-bedroom home close to his mom and mine. I was the happiest I had ever been in my life. When Lincoln told me that his mom was okay with the divorce and gave us her blessings, I was over the moon excited. My only wish was that Lincoln and I were married by the time I gave birth.

Josiah and Nova had gotten engaged and I was so happy for them. She was just as pregnant and fat as I was. I was extremely happy that she and I were able to share this experience together. It brought us even closer together.

Lincoln and Tiffani were finding a way to coexist as they prepared for the birth of their daughter. He was doing everything he could to get along with her, and so was she, but sometimes, she gave him a hard time. I tried to speak to her in a civilized manner, I mean, we're all adults, but she wanted nothing to do with me. She still considered me the homewrecker that stole her man. I didn't like her calling me that, but I couldn't make her stop.

One day she had called for Lincoln, but he was busy putting our baby's crib together. I looked at him and said, "It's your ex."

He rolled his eyes upward and asked, "Do you mind answering it for me?"

"Babe, now you know she don't want nothing to do with me."

"She ain't got a choice if I'm busy."

I didn't want to answer, but I did. "Hello Tiffani."

"Where's Lincoln?" she asked in a very rude tone.

"He's putting the baby's crib together."

"Well, can you give him the phone?"

"I can, but he asked what did you want."

"Tell him I need to speak with him… NOW!"

I just handed the phone to Lincoln because I was tired of her and her bitchy attitude. It wasn't my fault Lincoln wanted out of his marriage. He didn't blame me for their marriage ending, so why did she? I guess people could never take responsibility for their own shit. I mean, their marriage was over before I came back home, from what I understood.

She had been fighting a losing battle for a long time. "What Tiff?"

He was silent for a minute as he listened to her. "I put up our daughter's crib last week! My son needs a crib too! What do you want?"

More silence. "You're not in labor! The baby isn't due for another two months," he said.

More silence. "Well, I know you're not in labor from the attitude you had when I picked up. Go soak in the tub or something and I'll check on you tomorrow," he said and placed the phone down next to him.

"She's in labor, huh?" I asked.

"Man, I wish she wasn't pregnant. Every fuckin' day she tries to get me over there for something. I wish she would just grow the hell up!"

"She needs a man," I said.

"She sure does!" he said with a laugh.

He continued to fix the crib as I watched him. He was leaving for work next week, but he was only going to be gone fourteen days, so he could be back in time for our baby's birth. I was going to miss him so much. Once he was finished with the crib, he looked at me and said, "You are so beautiful."

I was sitting in the plush rocker by the window with my feet up on the ottoman. "Thank you, baby."

He kissed me softly on the lips and said, "Stay right here."

"Where are you going?" I asked.

"I'll be right back," he said.

I sat in the rocker, rocking back and forth while rubbing my protruding belly. Our son picked at that moment to start doing his somersaults.

Lincoln returned a short time later, looking all mysterious and shit. He sat on the ottoman in front of me and smiled. "You know I love you, right?"

"I do know that," I said as I returned his smile.

"I think that I've loved you since the first day we met, and you slapped me. I dreamed of living this life with you since the day you came back into my life. I have never loved anyone the way that I love you. I've never wanted to be with a woman as much as I've wanted you. You've given me unconditional love and my first son," he said as tears welled up in his eyes. I reached out and wiped them away. I didn't know where all of this was going, but I appreciated hearing how much he loved me. "I'm happier than I've ever been in my entire life, but there's only one thing in this whole world that would make me happier." He pulled his hand out from behind his back, revealing a little red velvet box.

He opened the box and inside was a beautiful princess cut diamond ring, with baguettes on each side. My mouth hit my lap with a thump. Tears welled up in my eyes as I stared at the gorgeous ring and the man I loved. He took the ring out of the box and said, "The only thing that would make me happier is if you agreed to become my wife. With that being said, will you marry me, bae?"

"Oh my God, baby! I do, I mean, I will, I mean… YES! A thousand times YES!" He placed the ring on my finger, grabbed both sides of my face, and kissed me deep and lovingly. Tears were streaming down both our faces by the time he had placed the ring on my finger.

When we pulled apart, I looked at him and my ring and said, "We're getting married. We're getting married."

"Hell yes!"

"I love you so much, Lincoln."

"I love you, too, Mrs. Smoke," he joked as we busted out laughing.

That night was the best night of my life, of our lives. Who knew that it was about to be marred by such a jealous woman…

Chapter seventeen

Tiffani

Three days later...

I was tired waiting for my husband, well ex-husband now, to come to his senses and come back to me. I wanted more than anything for this baby to bring him home to me, but that wasn't what happened. I had a feeling this baby wasn't my husband's and because I knew that I would get shunned if I confronted Josiah and Nova, I couldn't do that. What the hell was I supposed to do when my whole entire world had fell apart?

Everything was going right for them, but when was I going to get my happiness? I knew I should be happier about having a baby, but what woman wanted to have a baby alone? What woman wanted to be a single parent? I loved Lincoln and when I married him, I meant what I said about til death do us part, but he didn't. I saw that homewrecker and Nova posted their big bellies on Facebook. They were both due around the same time, and that hurt to see the pics of them all happy while I was dying inside.

I was going through their new pics when something caught my eye. I had to enlarge the pic to make sure I was seeing correctly. Oh, hell no! Lincoln had gave that bitch a ring! They were getting married. The ink had just dried on our divorce papers! Then he had the nerve to give her a ring that was bigger than mine. Oh, I forgot... he loved her. He didn't give a shit about me... but he would.

****

I knew that the bitch was in her last month of pregnancy, but I'd be damn if she ever gave birth. Lincoln had gone back to work yesterday, so I was gonna make sure I took care of his bitch for him. I had already made my peace with God and decided that I wasn't going to raise this child by myself. She was better off not being born. She should have never been brought into this situation in the first place.

As I watched the homewrecker leave their new home, I wondered where she was going. I didn't care where she was going because she wasn't going to make it there. As she made the right turn, I knew exactly where she would end up. I went around and timed my shit exact to meet up with her coming in the opposite direction.

As she approached the traffic light, which was red because it was also red on my side, I ran my red light, aiming straight for her. In the midst of my doing that, I didn't see the car coming on the opposite side of me, who had the right of way and the green light. He ran into my car, hitting my side door and part of the back door. As my car spun out of control, my only hope was that I ended up hitting that bitch's car. I heard the glass shattering around me and the metal twisting up as I screamed.

I felt the car stop, but I couldn't move. I felt the horrible pain in my legs and belly. As I looked down, I saw blood between my legs. I heard someone screaming as people began to approach my car. I could feel my face getting wet, so I moved my right arm to touch it. Blood was oozing from my face and everything hurt.

"Tiffani, don't move!" I heard that bitch say outside my window. My glass on my driver's side window was shattered and I wanted to turn my head, but I seriously couldn't move. I began to feel a tightening in my chest as I felt the horrendous pain coming from my pelvic region and back. I tried to speak, but no words would come.

"The paramedics are coming!" I heard someone yell. I didn't give a fuck about the damn paramedics. I wanted to get out of my car and choke that bitch where she stood.

"Ow!" I said as tears ran down my face, or maybe it was more blood. I could hear sirens in the distance, and more people being nosy. I could feel the life slipping out of me at the same time I heard someone say, "Don't worry, ma'am. We're gonna get you out of there!"

I just closed my eyes and waited for them to get me out. I swore that as soon as I felt better, I was coming for that bitch again. She would never be able to have a happy life as long as I was alive.

Chapter eighteen

Maddie

I was on my way to a doctor's appointment when it happened. I was approaching the red light at the intersection when this car came barreling through the red light on the opposite side. I didn't know what to do because the car was coming straight for me. Before I knew it, a car from the other side that had the green light slammed right into the car that was coming at me. I swear I saw my life flash before my eyes. I just knew that me and my baby were about to die.

Once the car stopped moving and I got a closer look at it, I could tell that it was Tiffani's car. "Oh my God!" I cried as I dialed 911.

"911, do you need fire, police, or ambulance?"

"There was an accident at the intersection of Bromwell and Corpus. Please hurry, it's really bad and the driver of the car that was hit is almost eight months pregnant!" I cried.

"The paramedics are already on the way, ma'am."

"Thank you! Please tell them to hurry!" I said in a panic. I slid out of my car and slowly made my way to Tiffani's car. I needed to check on her and make sure she was okay. "Tiffani, don't move. The paramedics are on the way!" I called out to her. She seemed to be in a lot of pain and unable to move.

Her car was messed up pretty badly. Her driver's side door was totally smashed in and there was some damage to the back door as well. I felt sorry for her and wondered why would she blow through that red light like that when she knew she was pregnant. Then it hit me... she wanted to hit me. She wanted to crash her car into mine. Oh my God! She wanted to kill me and my baby. Damn.

I got in my car and moved out of the line of traffic. I pulled to the side and waited to see where the ambulance was gonna go. I called Lincoln because I needed him to know what happened. He answered on the second ring, but we lost connection before I had a chance to say anything. I called back and hoped he was in a better area. Sometimes, he could get a good signal and sometimes he couldn't. I prayed this was the sometimes when he would have a signal because this was an emergency.

"Hello, bae are you alright?" he asked.

"I'm fine, but there's been an accident," I said.

"What? An accident? What happened? Is it my mom?"

I knew he was panicking, so I quickly said, "Your mom is fine. It's Tiffani!"

"Tiffani? What's wrong with Tiffani?"

"She got in a really bad car accident..." I said as I started to cry. I was trembling and shook up at the fact that my fiance's ex-wife wanted to kill me.

"Baby, are you okay? Is Tiffani okay?"

"Babe, she crashed right in front of me and no, she's hurt really bad!" I said.

I watched as the ambulance got on the road and said, "I'm following the ambulance to see which hospital they're taking her to. Come home, baby. Please."

"I'll be there, baby."

The connection died at that moment. Dammit!

I called Nova and explained to her what was going on. She said she would meet me at the hospital. When I pulled up behind the ambulance, I found a parking spot close to the door. I waddled my way over there just in time to see them pulling Tiffani out the back of the ambulance. One of the paramedics was pumping oxygen into her while they pushed her through. I didn't know who her mom was, so I had no way of knowing how to contact her.

I rushed in and approached the receptionist. "Ma'am, a woman was just brought in. Her name is Tiffani Hunter and she was involved in a car accident," I said.

"Are you related to her?" she asked.

"I'm Maddie Hunter, I need to know how is she," I asked.

Nova came waddling in at that moment. "How's Tiffani?" Nova asked.

"I don't know. I was waiting for this lady to tell me." I looked at the lady behind the desk with a smirk on my face.

"One moment," she said as she picked up the phone. "The family for the woman that was brought in is in the waiting room." She turned to us and said, "The doctor will be right out."

The two of us moved to the waiting room to wait for the doctor. About five minutes later, the doctor emerged from behind the double doors. "Tiffani Hunter's family!" he called.

We rushed as fast as our pregnant legs could carry us. "How is she, doctor? How's the baby?"

"I'm afraid we weren't able to save her or the baby. I'm sorry, but we did everything we could," the doctor said.

"Oh my God! She died?!" I asked.

"Yes, ma'am. The family will be able to claim her body in the morgue within the next 24-hours. Again, I'm sorry for your loss," he said as he disappeared behind the doors again.

Tears slid down my face. I didn't even know that I was crying until Nova said, "I can't believe that she's gone. Why are you crying? You know that girl ain't never liked you."

"I'm crying because she's dead. But the killing part of this whole thing is that I think she was gunning for me when she ran that red light." I said through my tears.

"What? Are you serious?"

"I was right at the light when she came barreling through. If it wasn't for that car hitting hers, I'd probably be just as dead as she is," I said.

Nova put her arms around me and we cried together. We decided to go over to Nova's house and send text messages to our men to let them know where we were. The two of us were so shook up that we ended up sleeping in Nova's bed. This had been one exhausting day...

Epilogue

Lincoln

Three months later...

I couldn't believe that Tiffani was dead. When I got the call from Maddie, I told Josiah and we took emergency leave from the rig. When Maddie explained to me that Tiffani was actually aiming for her when she sped through that red light, I thanked God that she wasn't successful with what she wanted to do. I didn't know what I would have done if I had lost Maddie and our baby boy. Tiffani wasn't the same person she was when I married her. I guess losing me pushed her over the edge.

Her mom wouldn't allow us to attend the funeral, but I still paid my respects. A couple of weeks after, my baby went into labor and gave birth to our beautiful baby boy. We named him Hakeem Lincoln Hunter and he was the spitting image of me, with the exception of his mom's little nose. As I watched her breastfeeding him, I admired her strength. She was the most beautiful mother I had ever seen, besides my own of course. Watching her with our son always made my heart skip two beats more than normal.

There wasn't a woman on this earth I loved more than Maddison Carter and in six months, I would make her my wife. I couldn't wait to call her Mrs. Maddison Hunter.

Maddie

I never saw what happened to Tiffani happening. I knew she was hurt and upset by her break up with Lincoln, but I didn't think it was that bad. She killed herself and her unborn child that day and it haunted me. To see a major accident like that happen in my face was just awful. Sometimes, I still had nightmares about that day.

What helps me pull through was the fact that I had my beautiful son and my amazing man. I couldn't wait to marry Lincoln in six months. He was the most wonderful father to Hakeem and I knew he would be a great husband. Nova and Josiah are also planning their wedding and she had a baby son. The four of us are closer than we had ever been. Nova confessed to me that she was the one who initially told Tiffani about Lincoln and me. I was upset with her for betraying me, but after everything that went down with Tiffani, I wasn't about to hold any grudges against my best friend.

What was done was done and our friendship was stronger because of it…

Josiah

I would be lying if I said that I was sad about Tiffani's passing. I cared about the girl, but her having a baby would have fucked up my entire equation. I loved Nova and she was the one for me. There was no way I was going to lose her behind no bullshit that Tiffani was trying to start. Of course, I felt bad that she had gotten killed, but I wasn't sad about it. That was one secret I was going to take to the grave.

I had way too much to lose by confessing that shit to Nova. We had a son together and were planning a wedding within the next year. She and my son meant everything to me. I was in love with my family. As happy as we were, there was nothing that could ever tear us apart now. Our shit was solid.

Nova

Tiffani's death hit everyone pretty hard. I mean, it just happened out of the blue and no one was expecting it. I felt so horrible about that happening to her, but I couldn't worry about that too much. A week after her death, I gave birth to my baby boy, who we named Joshua. He weighed 10 pounds 6 ounces and he tore my butt up.

My little boy and Josiah were the apples of my eye. I loved them more than life itself and there was nothing that could break us up. My family was the most important thing to me. Maddie and I were still the best of friends. She actually forgave me for telling Tiffani about her and Lincoln. I didn't think she would forgive me for that, but she did. She was and always would be my BFF.

We're now the four musketeers with babies in tow. My grandmother always said as long as you kept God first, everything else would fall into place. She was right. The four of us attend church every Sunday when the boys are home from work. When they're off, Maddie and I attend with the babies.

Our lives couldn't be more perfect...

Check Out Other Great Books From Tiece Mickens Presents

Please Save Me Before It's Too Late

Woman to Woman: It's Only Fair 3

But You Said You Loved Me

Rashad and Ayesha: Loving Blue Forever

Legend & Lyrical 2